Focused
for Bowling

Focused for Bowling

Dean Hinitz

Human Kinetics

Library of Congress Cataloging-in-Publication Data

Hinitz, Dean R.
    Focused for bowling / Dean Hinitz.
        p. cm.
Includes bibliographical references and index.
    ISBN 0-7360-3708-X (soft cover)
    1. Bowling--Psychological aspects. I. Title.
    GV903 .H56 2003
    794.6--dc21

                                                    2002005931

ISBN: 0-7360-3708-X

Copyright © 2003 by Dean Hinitz

Acquisitions Editor: Todd Jensen; **Developmental Editor:** Cynthia McEntire; **Assistant Editor:** John Wentworth; **Copyeditor:** Patsy Fortney; **Proofreader:** Myla D. Smith; **Indexer:** Craig Brown; **Graphic Designer:** Nancy Rasmus; **Graphic Artist:** Francine Hamerski; **Photo Manager:** Leslie A. Woodrum; **Cover Designer:** Keith Blomberg; **Photographer (cover):** Leslie A. Woodrum; **Photographer (interior):** Leslie A. Woodrum unless otherwise noted; **Art Manager:** Carl D. Johnson; **Illustrator:** Brian McElwain; **Printer:** United Graphics

Human Kinetics books are available at special discounts for bulk purchase. Special editions or book excerpts can also be created to specification. For details, contact the Special Sales Manager at Human Kinetics.

Printed in the United States of America   10 9 8 7 6 5 4 3 2 1

Human Kinetics
Web site: www.HumanKinetics.com

United States: Human Kinetics
P.O. Box 5076
Champaign, IL 61825-05076
800-747-4457
e-mail: humank@hkusa.com

Canada: Human Kinetics
475 Devonshire Road Unit 100
Windsor, ON N8Y 2L5
800-465-7301 (in Canada only)
e-mail: orders@hkcanada.com

Europe: Human Kinetics
107 Bradford Road
Stanningley
Leeds LS28 6AT, United Kingdom
+44 (0) 113 255 5665
e-mail: hk@hkeurope.com

Australia: Human Kinetics
57A Price Avenue
Lower Mitcham, South Australia 5062
08 8277 1555
e-mail: liahka@senet.com.au

New Zealand: Human Kinetics
P.O. Box 105-231, Auckland Central
09-523-3462
e-mail: hkp@ihug.co.nz

To my father, David, who taught me about unflinching integrity and commitment to the right action. To my mother, Marcia, who gave me the tools and caring to move in a world that contained other people. To my wife, April, who has held my hand through the darkest and lightest moments. And to my son, David, who keeps me true to who I say I am.

contents

foreword

As a child in Alaska, I played a variety of sports. Most kids learned how to ice skate, for obvious reasons, and then took up hockey. During the brief summers, baseball was very popular. But as fate would have it, my father owned a bowling center, so bowling captured my imagination more than anything else.

I really don't remember being in situations as a youngster that required me to perform in the 10th frame. Perhaps it was because I hadn't perfected a style that allowed me to repeat shots at the level that one must possess on the PBA tour. The first time I remember feeling real pressure was when I joined a men's league while a senior in high school. For the first time, I could get money, win recognized tournaments, and realize my accomplishments with real stuff.

In 1976, I was bowling in the state tournament and badly wanted to win the state all-events title. If I succeeded, I would win a trip to a national roll-off against all the other winners. I started off in the team event and did poorly. I knew I needed to bowl extremely well in the doubles and singles to have any chance. A good score had already been posted. The general feeling was that whoever passed that score eventually would win. During the doubles event, I felt a momentum shift. It was easy then, just chasing a score. I finished shooting around 750.

Next all I had to do to win was bowl pretty well in the singles. During the singles, I still felt the momentum as I continued the chase. As the last game began, I knew exactly what score I had to beat. I also knew exactly what it felt like to experience real pressure . . . *real* pressure. Knowing that it was all on the line, knowing that everyone else knew it was all on the line, I felt like everyone in the world was watching me and I was the only one who mattered. I did not like that feeling. It did things to my stomach that I wasn't used to.

I eventually bowled a game good enough to win, although in retrospect it was a mediocre one. I believe it was necessary for me to work through those feelings in order to learn to excel. To this day, I still have to manage my feelings in competition. I can honestly say that even though I have accomplished more than most bowlers imagine, I still have to learn to manage my excitement during high-stakes competition. It is a neverending process. To overcome it and never feel the competition demons would make one immortal. Everybody, although some will not admit it, feels pressure at times. It is the art of managing feelings that is an ingredient of greatness.

In my travels, I frequently am asked the secret to my success. It is easy for me to convey my thoughts on this. However, it is much more difficult for me to answer when I am asked about achieving mental toughness. Every bowler is different. I know what goes on in my mind, and what has gone on in my own memories. I don't know what goes on in someone else's mind. I don't know the infinite complexities of how others process information, only what I have figured out about winning.

During my first semester of college I took a course called "Introduction to Logic." I still use these basic principles of logic. If P then Q. If not P then Q. If P then not Q. And finally if not P then not Q. Let me explain this in simple bowling terms. If I work hard, then I will get better. If I do not work hard, then I will not get better. If I practice more, I will get better. If I do not practice, then I will not get better. If I believe that I can win, then I will win. If I think that I cannot win, then I will not win.

If you ask yourself a logical question about your level of commitment, and you intuitively or rationally know that you are not giving it your best effort, then your conscious as well as your subconscious mind knows it. I believe that a part of your subconscious guides you through life's tests and trials. Failure to do the things you know would make you a better person, a better athlete, or a contributing member of society prevents you from achieving your ultimate goals. Does this have anything to do with performing in the 10th frame? I believe it does. You cannot move forward in life until you really listen to yourself. This is the best single piece of advice I can give to anyone—listen to yourself!

I believe champion athletes show similarities in their ingredients for success. Some of these factors are obvious. Confidence, will power, desire, relentlessness, perseverance, work ethic, and sacrifice immediately come to mind. Most success boils down to commitment and attitude. The most difficult part of a success formula to define is the mental game.

I think of concentration as the art of not thinking. Concentration is knowing the task at hand and simply executing it. Knowing where to stand, where to look, and how to roll the ball is all that is needed to make excellent shots. If I can eliminate all other thoughts, I have the best chance of doing well. However, mastering the art of not thinking is not a simple skill to achieve. My objective in competition is to achieve a state of mind where I direct my thoughts to three essentials—the location of my feet, my visual focus, and my intention concerning how I plan to roll the ball. In addition, I sometimes make a conscious effort to monitor my heart beat. I like to feel as if I am in control of my own pulse rate. Does my heart rate elevate in pressure situations? Sure, but not as much as it would if I did not practice a regulation technique.

When you watch bowling, enjoy heroic efforts. Do not revel in your competitors' failures. Show humility when you watch others. Separate yourself from those who want to share misery and choose a path that will allow for heroics. Great duals require worthy competition. When you experience defeat, still show genuine happiness for your competitor. Tomorrow could be your day to win. Accept that it can never be your day all the time. Every competition experience is a step on the path to greatness. This attitude is essential to ultimately winning.

It is said that confidence breeds confidence, and that winning breeds winning. The single most important hurdle to conquer is winning for the first time. Other hurdles appear after that first one, but it seems like everything you do is to get over that that first big one. Sadly, only the great ones clear this barrier. Without making that jump, the rewards of your labor may remain hidden in terms of sports success. I say hidden, not lost, because they are there, needing only to be discovered.

I am a God-fearing man. I believe that my perspective on life eased the pressure of achieving greatness in my sport. From my point of view, my bowling accomplishments pale in comparison to my overall objectives in life. If my values and perspective were different, I would not have accomplished all that I have. I have used my experiences to learn things about life that are far more important than national titles.

I have described *my* recipe for greatness. You must figure out what makes up your recipe. That is what this book is for! You cannot get bread to rise without adding in the essential ingredients. It is time for you to find yours.

Brian Voss

acknowledgments

I never really grasped the importance of acknowledgment pages until I finished this book. The reality is that this book is the culmination of attention, support, instruction, mentoring, and aid that I have received in innumerable places. To bypass the opportunity to recognize special people in my life would be to pretend that I have somehow completed this book, or done anything else of note, without priceless contributions from friends and family. On the other hand, much like working on a wedding invitation list, I could never include everyone who has touched me and influenced this work.

I would like to first acknowledge the professional and amateur bowlers with whom I have been privileged to work. Oddly enough, because of the nature of our work together and my confidentiality agreements, I am not at liberty to identify any of them by name. You have certainly been my teachers as much as I have been yours. I also wish to recognize Cynthia McEntire, my editor and consultant at Human Kinetics. She coached, supported, and directed in ways that left me motivated with my self-esteem still intact.

There are a host of bowling personalities, coaches, and mentors who walked me through a great deal of what does and does not work in the mental and physical aspects of bowling. I am indebted to the gang at High Sierra Lanes in Reno, coach Ron Bruner, Rudy and Donovan Moreno, Ron and Tori Krys, Richard Baldo, Ron Morehead, Jerry Netherton, and Steve Mikkelson. Thank you to the players and teachers I competed with and against in order to develop my bowling skills and the source material for this book. I truly hope you recognize yourselves here.

Chris Alderucci was my first bowling coach and a resource treasure in the world of bowling. Ray Blanchard and Bettie Spruill taught me how to turn life into an experiential exercise and gave me the skills to design learning for others. Susie Minshew has been a great partner to work with across time and distance. My father-in-law, Nick Bay, is money in the bank when it comes to the kind of advice sons need from dads when they are involved in projects. Thank you to my sisters Jill and Connie for leading by example and blazing a trail that I could follow. Steve Graybar has been with me shoulder to shoulder as we each tilted at our particular windmills.

And finally, I am grateful to Bob Summerville, who taught me how to write as if we were having a beer together, instead of presenting to a dissertation committee.

introduction

The View From the Top

Here it is. This is the situation some athletes dream of and other athletes dread. All you need is to mark in the 10th to win the tournament. Strike, and it is iced. Perhaps the television cameras are focusing in on your face. At the very least your opponent and the fans are paying close attention.

If you are a mentally tough bowler, you clear the distractions, harness your emotions, recall your focus plan, and deliver an elegant shot. If you are a mentally soft bowler, you are bothered that it all comes down to this. You feel a hitch in your confidence about executing the shot. Thoughts about the consequences of making or missing the shot hover like cartoon demons. You deliver the shot tightly, mechanically. If the ball strikes, you feel as though you did it with smoke and mirrors as opposed to skill and heart.

But what if you don't strike? Perhaps the 6-pin wraps the 10, leaving the 10 standing there like a soldier guarding the corner of the lane. You are now in an another high-pressure situation. If you are a mentally tough bowler, you handle this shot exactly as you handled the previous one. Your plan is set. Your delivery is flawless. You shoot the spare just as you expected. If you are a mentally soft bowler, however, you become angry that the 10-pin stuck. You waste time wishing and hoping instead of feeling secure about shooting the spare.

These are money shots. This is where the rubber meets the road in terms of who has game, or in other words, who is mentally tough. When you think of mentally tough bowlers, who comes to mind? Perhaps you think of the bowlers of yore such as Dick Weber and Earl Anthony, or recent champions such as Norm

Courtesy of Kim terrell.

Recent champion Kim Terrell is an example of a mentally tough bowler. In 2002, she struck in the 10th frame to win the Queens Championship and back-to-back major titles.

Duke, Walter Ray Williams, Carolyn Dorin-Ballard, or Kim Terrell. Maybe someone who bowls in leagues or tournaments closer to home epitomizes the mentally tough bowler to you. In any case, what is it about these bowlers that indicates mental strength— the fact that they win? Actually, that's only part of the equation. Although mentally strong athletes often do win, what distinguishes them from the wimps is far more than that. These athletes possess a combination of the following factors.

A mentally strong bowler can *channel and redirect nervous energy*. Curiously, the key to a good game is not avoiding or preventing nervousness but rather delivering good shots despite nervousness or tension. A common fallacy is that a strong mental game requires an icy nervous system. You are supposed to feel something when you compete! Sport psychology focuses so much on controlling breathing, pulse, and excitement level that sometimes athletes get nervous simply because they experience intense feelings. Intense feelings are part of what makes bowling worth doing. Competition adds some juice to life. Attempting to numb your nerves will turn you into a robot. Champions learn to bowl no matter what their energy levels, without being highly invested in changing them. Oddly enough, this shift in priorities often serves to calm the nerves automatically.

A mentally strong bowler knows how to *focus*. Nothing takes away from the bowler's getting into the flow of the shot—not high (or low) stakes, not TV cameras or noisy spectators. Like a cat stalking a bird, once the preliminary stages of getting ready to bowl have begun, the bowler goes into an action sequence that is unshakable. Even in practice, champion bowlers bring so much awareness to the immediate shot that they can achieve maximum skill execution and optimal learning from the results. Bowlers who do not have this quality get lazy or minimize the importance of every shot. The result is a lower learning curve and more surprises in competitive situations. Always remember, there are no throwaway moments in bowling!

The mentally strong bowler who gets distracted or throws a bad shot or low game *recovers* in a heartbeat and gets right back into a focused mental state and optimal physical performance. The only benefit to thinking about a bad shot or ball reaction is to learn from it. Champions realize that the only shot that matters is the next one. If they must correct their timing or execution, they do so. They don't waste energy grieving the missed spare or the poorly thrown shot that leaves a pin in the back row or worse.

The mentally tough bowler knows about delivering the goods in any situation. Bowling occurs with *economy of thought and an open channel of flow*. Internally a warm flood of confidence goes with the thought "I know I will." A clear body–mind connection exists, allowing the bowler to deliver beautiful shots in pressure-packed situations. Instead of thinking about the mechanics of how to deliver the ball or how to make a spare, the bowler experiences the whole sequence as one continuous movement. Bowlers who don't have this ability tend to entertain creeping doubts at critical times. They get stiff or rigidly methodical when the pressure builds. In the worst cases, the ball, the body, and the shot are all disconnected. Once doubts begin to take hold, mental overthinking can keep bowlers from regaining the naturalness that is the art of bowling.

The mentally strong bowler *accepts feedback*, taking and profiting from observations and coaching from others. An athlete who can integrate information from knowledgeable observers demonstrates confidence, intelligence, and a sense of security. The ability to make adjustments in the mental and physical game based on input is a hallmark of a championship, continuous improvement process. Some athletes take any input as criticism, whereas others think they know so much that they discount information from others. A lack of appreciation for the feedback of others and an inability to use that feedback will delay or even freeze improvement. When the only view is the one inside your own head, it can be a narrow picture.

The mentally strong bowler can *keep cool*. Even when leaving an unusual or *unfair* spare like a split, the big four, or a ringing 10-pin, the champion bowler maintains composure. The game does not melt down. There is no substitute for getting right back in the game and throwing good, solid shots.

Many competitors belong to the "life should be fair" school of bowling. They think that if they throw a shot properly, only good things should happen. Bowlers who understand the absolute impartiality of the pins, the lanes, and the game may be disappointed that they didn't score, but they don't spend much time or energy bemoaning the last shot. Champions of the mental game note anything that they need to learn and move on quickly to the next frame.

Whether ahead or behind in the game, the mentally strong bowler *stays motivated* and bowls wholeheartedly. Interest in the game rarely waivers, and each shot is treated as important, even when the bowler is many points ahead or behind the opponent or tournament cut line. All competitive athletes face the risk of playing up or down to the level of the competition. However, the path of excellence should not depend on how other athletes fare. Champions call forth the best in themselves in all competitive situations, no matter how others are doing. Mental training dictates that all shots delivered in competitive situations are training for future shots. Mentally tough bowlers never allow their competitive minds to slow down and become dull and disinterested. They are convinced of the value of all performance situations.

The mentally strong bowler *stays in the present* and bowls each shot as though it were the only shot that ever existed. He or she does not waste time and energy complaining about, or celebrating, past performances or worrying about what's coming next. Getting caught up in past and future successes and failures is only food for the ego. Living in past victories or losses can leave a sweet or bitter taste in the mouth, but it doesn't generate anything new. Those victories won't provide a bye in the qualifying rounds of the next tournament. The losses don't prohibit winning from ever happening. Spending mental energy on the importance of the next shot, game, or tournament usually only escalates tension. Every moment, every shot, and every game should be treated as an independent event. The better you learn to live each shot in the present moment, the more training and skill you can bring to bear at crunch time.

Even after making an obvious error, such as throwing the ball into the channel or missing a single-pin spare, the mentally strong bowler *does not blow composure*. The champion bowler pulls the mental and emotional package together quickly and goes right back to throwing good shots. Champions of the mental game stay away from all-or-nothing, black-or-white thinking. They don't believe that their games or their bowling are defined by any one shot. One missed shot or open frame doesn't blow everything in a career or a life. Mentally tough bowlers minimize concerns about what others will think. Instead they focus on whatever comes next.

This is the view from the peak of the mental game mountain. At this point, you don't have to know exactly how to get there. That is the purpose of this book! However, you do have to be able to assess where you currently stand. In chapter 1 you will have a chance to evaluate where you are in your mental game by walking through some self-assessment exercises. This is a critical part of every bowler's development. Moving ahead without self-evaluation is like trying to groom for the prom without looking in a mirror. It can be done, but it is so much more work and leaves too much room to miss essential details.

The remainder of the book is designed to take you, the committed bowler, through the mental muscle development that can open up a world-class mental game, no matter what level of the physical game you have achieved.

Chapter 2 is about groundbreaking vision in terms of goal setting and accomplishment. In this chapter you will have the opportunity to take a realistic look at where you are, where you intend to go, and how you will measure the journey. You will discover the mind-set and techniques that distinguish the goal achiever from the average New Year's resolution maker. Here you will learn the kind of commitment required to develop the iron will that is part of a spectacular mental game.

Chapter 3 outlines the essential ingredients and design of an effective preshot routine. You will learn how the preshot routine works and how to create one that travels easily from tournament to tournament, no matter where it is.

Chapter 4 focuses on managing excitement and other emotions to execute shots under any conditions. This chapter is a buffet table from which you can take whatever works for you. Because individuals differ greatly in how they respond to attempts to handle high-intensity situations, this chapter offers a variety of approaches to succeeding under any circumstances. From self-talk to breathing to muscle relaxation, chapter 4 is a smorgasbord from which to choose.

Chapter 5 is about developing the psychological muscle to deal with all kinds of competition adversity. Whether you get distracted by noise, other bowlers, a television crew, or your internal emotions, you need a strategy for what to do when something pulls you out of flow. You will learn to focus and concentrate no matter what is going on mentally, emotionally, or in the bowling center.

"Strike for show, spare for dough" is the mantra of the competitive bowler. Perfect games are wonderful to experience. However, just about anyone who has missed the cut in a tournament or been barely beaten in match play can blame a blown spare. Effective mental and physical game strategy for shooting spares adds a great deal of confidence to any bowler. Chapter 6 will take you on this journey to the promised land called great spare shooting.

The truly committed bowler walks the fine line between disciplined training and burnout. Burnout is an overtraining virus that can result in boredom with the game, fatigue, irritability, and stale performance. Chapter 7 addresses the signs, symptoms, prevention, and cure for burnout. Chapter 7 provides a compass you can use to navigate the potholes and risks that can send you to the burnout dungeon.

Chapter 8 deals with slumps. Every bowler has highs and lows, often on the same day. Slumps are those periods when you feel stuck and lost; you feel as though you are getting worse . . . and it goes on for days, maybe even weeks or longer. This chapter is about breaking free without breaking down. Diagnosis and recovery plans should turn this syndrome into nothing more than the common cold of bowlers.

Chapter 9 is about mastery. Mastery means pulling together all the pieces that make up a superior mental game. This chapter is a summary of the mind-set, training tools, and behaviors you need to practice to reach the heights in this sport. Now you get to see what you can really do. This chapter is about excellence of the highest order, a rewarding conclusion to the journey this book invites you to take.

chapter

1

SELF-
ASSESSMENT
AND
EVALUATION

Talking in general terms about the mental game—in any sport—is like talking to an Eskimo about snow. An Eskimo knows dozens of words for different kinds of snow: *icy, wet, powdery,* and so on. Simply saying there is snow is too general a statement. The same is true for the mental game. The mental game can involve relaxation, focus, visualization, and much more.

Mental game work is more than just managing feelings, practicing techniques, and controlling muscles. Having a strong mental game means being able to call forth your best qualities when you need them—in the heart of competition, for example. It is like having a warrior within to assist you whenever necessary.

Some athletes master the mental game, and some never do. Just like the physical aspects of bowling, mastery of the mental game requires practice. Once you have achieved that mastery, you can call on your mental warrior when striving for excellence or when the chips are down and pressure is high. Master actualizing your competitive self, and the bowling world will be yours for the taking.

The next portion of this chapter is critical to developing an understanding of the central concepts of mental toughness. This understanding will strengthen the application of every other part of this book.

Waking the Warrior

Every bowler has multiple personalities, not the made-for-TV-movie kinds, but rather different mind-sets in practice, competition, and outside-life situations. Competitive bowlers bring confidence, nervousness, excitement, fear, and other reactions to every league or tournament outing. Unfortunately, bowlers often are unable to control which reactions they generate on game day.

You may feel as though aspects of your competitive personality come and go based on the situation instead of your own choice or will. You don't have to live this way. In this book I invite you to wake the warrior inside and train it to come forth whenever needed. By learning an essential skill—the call to the competition self—you will be able to summon feelings related to flow, the zone, and bowling unconsciously.

Much of sport psychology teaches relaxing, calming nerves, and focusing attention. These interventions have great merit and proven results. However, sometimes they can be like raking leaves by climbing up into the tree when ground level is the place to be.

There are two deeper issues that have to be addressed about sports psychology interventions. The first is to examine what in the bowler's thinking creates nervousness, distraction, or lack of focus. The second is whether it is more effective to attack the symptoms of tension and pressure or to shift attention to other powerful confidence-building techniques when there is a lot riding on a shot or a game.

When champion bowlers talk privately about how they feel during successful bowling, they use words such as *relaxation, confidence, energy, joy,* and *satisfaction.* On poor bowling days, they talk about nervousness, tension, pointing shots, and frustration and anger. Some bowlers believe that their feelings depend on the whims of chance and the circumstances of life. They cannot explain why they have exceptional games on some days and weak games on others. It is almost as though some cosmic ray zaps them with good energy or bad energy, and that's what they are stuck with. The idea that they can have total control over their competitive state of mind is unfathomable to these bowlers. This is unfortunate, since champion bowlers have shown that taking ownership of both body and mind can mean the difference between a physically proficient but flat performance and an inspired one.

Competitors often get so wrapped up in trying not to feel nervous or scared and trying to feel calm and controlled that they completely miss the point of effective performance. Championship-quality performance does not depend on calmness, excitement, super energy, or even who has the biggest hand on the ball. The X-factor is *who you are* at the line.

Athletes sometimes feel uncomfortable if they cannot slow the adrenaline in their systems. Adrenaline is not the enemy, however. When athletes are performing well, adrenaline is commonly activated. Athletes shortchange themselves when they spend too much mental effort and energy trying to calm their physical and emotional systems when the competitive engines are revved.

There is a lot of good news about adrenaline rushes. They keep you awake, alert, and motivated when the stakes are high. Adrenaline is the juice that lends excitement and feelings of joy and accomplishment to competition. Finally, adrenaline can be used to create powerful pin fall action. Think of adrenaline as pure energy. It can serve as a potent ingredient in successful shot results.

Simply put, bowling is the process of allowing energy to move through the body, through the arm, off the fingertips, and into the ball. The ball carries that energy all the way to the pins. The more energy the ball has left inside it, the more a reaction can be expected to occur when the ball smacks the pins. A simple visualization process, addressed in chapter 6, will give you the recipe for making this work.

Think of feelings as body weather. Sometimes the weather is pleasant and sunny, sometimes it is stormy, but it is always changeable. Just as you prefer to perform outdoor activities in pleasant weather, we all prefer to compete when our thoughts and feelings are comfortable. Take this bowling analogy, for example. Imagine that you are at a tournament in an old, run-down bowling center (not such a stretch for many of us!). The air conditioning is bad and blows hot and cold sporadically. The ventilation is clogged so that even the smokers are getting queasy. The noise from the bar is deafening. You don't leave because the money is so good, or the title means something to you, or you simply love to bowl. For whatever reason, you are staying with the intention to bowl well. If you spend time and energy trying to get the management to fix the air conditioner or asking the people in the bar to keep it down, you will only experience frustration and distraction. If you accept the nature of the bowling center environment, these irritants may still be in the background of your consciousness, but you'll stop noticing them. Just like living next to a train station, when you give up trying to change the situation, you stop noticing the noise.

Fears, anxieties, and adrenaline are like internal mental and physical environmental factors. If you spend a lot of time and energy attempting to change your feelings, you will lose the focus on your shots. Worse yet, you may come to believe that something is wrong simply because you have not been able to harness all your thoughts and feelings. In fact, the more you try to fix your feelings, the more frustrated you may become.

While the basics of systematic breathing and other relaxation techniques can be quite useful, another factor, when mastered, can be even more effective and powerful: the personality factor. You are never stuck with one mode of operation. Consider the fact that you behave and feel quite differently at church, at the convenience store, or at the bowling center than you do at work. Different characteristics of your personality show up in different situations. The same is true about various competition settings and circumstances.

Table 1.1 shows some of the thoughts, feelings, and personality qualities that tend to emerge in relation to success and failure. A review of the table reveals a couple of important points. Choking, tensing, and tightening are directly related to focusing on the consequences of success and failure. This is past- and future-oriented thinking. Flow and success, on the other hand, are related to staying in the present moment and trusting only in oneself, not in the outcome. You experience joy when you feel masterful with your bowling. The goal is always full-potential bowling, which leads to great bowling outcomes and basic all-around happiness.

The $50,000 question (sometimes literally in bowling) is how to bowl with full potential. The answer is *pure intention*. The

TABLE 1.1 COMPARISON OF FEELINGS AND EMOTIONS RELATED TO FAILURE AND SUCCESS

Choking and failed performance	Full-potential bowling
Carefulness	Heart
Perfectionism	Passion and excellence
Aiming	Focus on execution
Tense, flexed muscles	Free flow of muscles and armswing
Fear of making a mistake	Guts
Wanting and wishing	Trust in self to bring it all
Anger and frustration about past shots	Totally present attitude
Past-oriented thinking about games	Totally present awareness
Needing/having to make a shot	Suspension of awareness of past and future consequences
Desperation	Joy

reason more bowlers don't choose the right thoughts, feelings, and results is that in their hearts they do not believe they have a choice. You always have a choice regarding your thoughts and feelings and letting it all go. Letting it go means that, live or die, you put all of yourself on the line, with no place to hide from outside observation or inside judgment and feelings. Remember this: Pure intention is the sword that cuts through the fog of a distracted or nervous mind.

You Are Whom You Choose to Be

You can pull together everything positive and good at critical moments. One of the purposes of this book is to help you create the confidence that helps you know that you really can roll a great ball under any circumstances. It is completely possible to integrate your thoughts, feelings, and physical stroke at the most crucial moments. Imagine our favorite scenario. You are in the heat of competition, about to throw a shot. Perhaps it is the first shot of the game or a spare in the 10th frame. Maybe the TV lights are coming back on after a commercial. Ask yourself one profound question: Who will I be when I deliver this shot? Not, "How will I feel?" but "Who will I be?"

A thousand answers may come to mind. Here are two possibilities: I am a careful, cautious, wanting, needing, overaiming person who rushes, worries, and tries to be perfect; or, I am a go-for-it, courageous battler who brings great heart, boldness, and intention to the game as I stay completely in the present.

Who do you want to sit down with after the shot? What memories do you want to fall asleep with? Generally you will be either a giver or a withholder. After you roll the shot and come back to sit down, ask yourself which one you were.

This does not mean being fake. It does mean finding something within you to lock onto on command. A real-world example of this would be if someone threatened a member of your family. You wouldn't have any trouble calling up aggression or assertiveness, even if those traits are not common and normal for you. Or if you saw a child fall from a bicycle and get hurt, you would feel concern, care, and empathy, even if you were in a hurry. Those feelings are easy and natural.

In bowling you can summon any qualities you choose to own and exhibit. You are shooting for the greatest, grandest, fullest expression of who you are as a person . . . while bowling. The challenge is to decide what aspects of yourself you will express on every shot—heart and complete effort, or something less. This is your choice every time.

Circumstances do not change what you can call forth from the warrior within. When the TV cameras come on, no change in plan. When a mark is needed to shut out an opponent, no change in plan. You must trust that your game will not get worse when you bring full heart and intention to the moment.

Decide whether you like the person who just rolled the ball, regardless of the pin fall. To test your intention, imagine a thin curtain set up 50 feet down the lane that keeps you from seeing the result of your shot. After rolling the ball, you know what you brought to the attempt, even without knowing whether the shot carried all 10 pins. Again, when the pressure is on, you always know whether you executed with heart and guts, or carefulness and overcontrol. The acid test is to ask yourself whether you would autograph a particular effort and release at the line, and answer yourself truthfully.

It takes a special kind of person to willingly put it all on the line. It means giving up pointing and perfection. It means not paying attention to the meaning of a missed shot. More than anything, it means actively choosing to define yourself as a warrior athlete who connects head with heart and leaves it all out there on the approach. Are you willing to put it all out there in front of teammates and viewing audiences? This is an important question that you must answer authentically.

It is hoped that most of the time you strike. Sometimes you spare. Rarely you miss. Regardless of the results, you must live with the person who rolled the ball. If you feel like a chicken, then when you do well you will feel relief rather than satisfaction. This will not improve your confidence. If you bring everything you have, guts and all, then no matter what happens 60 feet down the lane, you can say "that was all I had" and mean it. That is what it means to bowl with maximum excellence.

Three Steps to Confidence

Confidence can come either from results or from within. When you depend on results, you have to see a good ball reaction before trusting your technique. You have to have titles before believing in yourself and your ability to win future competitions. Confidence from within comes from trusting yourself, pure and simple. When you master internal trust, you will have complete faith in what you bring as an athlete; everything else is basically skill development. Here is a three-step model to achieve self-confidence.

Step 1 is deciding what physical and personal qualities you will bring to each shot. Physical qualities include hand position, ball speed and path, and finishing position. Personal qualities include guts, intensity, and passion. These lead to commitment to arm-swing and eagle eyes on the mark. To identify these qualities, think of a time when you were at your best, whether bowling or doing something else. Identify the qualities you manifested at that time and adapt them to the present task. This can be part of phase 1 (planning and intention) of the shot cycle (see chapter 4).

Step 2 is execution. Here you keep your word to yourself to follow through with your plan, or not. When you succeed with step 1, your self-confidence shoots to the moon. You no longer have to rely on results to trust your execution plan. Practice doing what you say you will do, regardless of circumstances. Attack with intention, allow for free armswing and follow-through, and enjoy the thrill of bringing it all together. This step correlates with phase 2 (execution and commitment) of the shot cycle.

Step 3 is maintaining an honest reflection of what you brought to the task and how it felt to roll each shot and game; essentially, in this step you reflect on who you were. When you bring your absolute best, whatever that is on a given day, life feels great. In so doing, you create the conditions for bowling, and living, to the maximum. You also reinforce great shot-making habits.

Many people believe that confidence comes from good results. In reality, confidence is born out of learning to trust oneself; it comes from knowing that you will bring all your skill and training to bear under any circumstance. Oil patterns, TV cameras, and disruptive competitors cannot take away this personal treasure.

Commit to excellence in execution and follow-through. You gain confidence by bringing all you have.

When you trust yourself enough to know that you will manifest boldness, passion, intention, and other positive qualities, your confidence will increase with each repetition. Great results will follow from the assuredness and execution that create those results.

Remember, to be effective in this process, you must be absolutely oriented to the present moment during every shot. Thinking about past mistakes or game finishes will kick you out of the moment. Likewise, thoughts about the consequences of hitting or missing a shot keep you from accessing and executing from your highest and best athletic expression.

Past- and future-oriented thinking can lead to agitation. Get clear. Get present. Decide what you intend to express; then keep your word to yourself and roll with authority. In the end, you have to like the bowler who rolled the shot. If you do not, winning won't build confidence. It will only provide periodic relief. No sport psychology technique is separate from the athlete who executes it. Go to the roots, not to the leaves, and decide who you are going to be.

Self-Evaluation

Imagine you are flying to Las Vegas. The plane develops trouble with the electronics systems, and all of the gauges and dials go blank. Fortunately, the pilot is able to land the plane safely in the desert. After a quick check to make sure everyone is OK, the pilot informs you that you are not too far from the city, but because the instrument panel is broken, he can't give more specific information.

To get where you need to go, you need to have only a few essential pieces of information: where you are, where Las Vegas is in relation to where you are, and how far you have to go. All three pieces of information are vital if you and your fellow passengers are going to find your way. The same is true of learning to master the mental game in bowling. You must know where you are, what your goals are, and how you will achieve them. This book is designed as a compass, a map, and a guide to help you do all three. You, of course, are both the driver and the engine.

This section will give you an opportunity to find out where you stand in relation to where you intend to go.

Where You Are

Imagine that you are in the settee area with a unique view of a special bowler—you. You can adopt two unique views. One is from the inside out—you have knowledge of hopes, fears, wishes, memories, and goals. The other is from the outside—you can see the history of actions and behaviors that have led to this point in your bowling career. These special insights make you the only person in the world who can truthfully answer the questions you will be asked in this section. Answering authentically will provide a good look in the mirror. This alone can serve as your wake-up call for what is solid in your mental game and what you need to improve. This assessment will also be something you can refer back to in order to make a continual appraisal of your mental game fitness.

Finding out where you are means stepping outside yourself and looking objectively at your bowling.

The self-assessment questionnaire shown in table 1.2 will help you determine where you are on the path to mastery of the mental game. Read each of the 10 statements and indicate if the statement is least true for you (1) or most true for you (5). Be completely honest, even if you don't care for the number you have to select. Self-improvement is much more likely if you are willing to be honest with yourself. In addition to being a measure of mental game fitness, this will be a test of how willing you are to give yourself real feedback.

Now let's see where you stack up in comparison with other athletes. In other sports, top-quality athletes have scores of 40 or higher on a scale similar to this one (Orlick 1980). If you scored about 40, you probably have some good mental competition muscle tone. For a strong mental game, you want to be in the 4-to-5-point range on each of the 10 items.

Take a look at your numbers. The places where you have 4s and 5s are mental game strengths. This does not mean you should leave these alone! Just as someone who is a great spare shooter needs to keep this skill sharp, so it is with the strongest aspects of your mental game.

If you have a 1, 2, or 3 on any of the items, there is great news here. You have identified where you will want to focus your attention. The other great news is that you don't have to stay there, and you will have a way to measure your own success over time. You also have company. Many of the professional male and female champions I have worked with had low numbers on one or more of these items. Mastery of their weaknesses is what allowed them to master their game and achieve consistently high performance. You can do the same and learn to excel as well as the legends do.

Where You Want to Go

Seeing where you are strong and where you are weak is only half the battle. To become a mentally strong bowler, you also have to commit to working on a program designed to help you succeed.

Most so-so, average, run-of-the-mill athletes do what they feel like doing. They may say they are going to practice three times a week, or work on corner spares, or run three miles a week, but they only follow through if they feel like it. If they are bored, tired, hungry, or discouraged, they tend to do something else. This

TABLE 1.2 MENTAL STRENGTH SELF-ASSESSMENT QUESTIONNAIRE

Read the 10 statements and choose a number from 1 to 5 that most closely represents your own experience. A 1 means the statement is least true for you. A 5 means the statement is most true.

STATEMENT	FALSE				TRUE
1. I don't choke from nervousness or tension during competition.	1	2	3	4	5
2. When I am throwing a shot, everything in the background goes away for me.	1	2	3	4	5
3. When I practice, I am very good at keeping strong motivation and focus.	1	2	3	4	5
4. Throughout competitions, whether league or tournament, I hold onto my focus. Attention and motivation stay strong.	1	2	3	4	5
5. When I compete, I start and stay confident. I know that I can repeat what I was able to do in practice.	1	2	3	4	5
6. I listen to my fellow bowlers and coaches when they have something to tell me. I don't get defensive. I can use what they tell me and apply it to my game when the information fits.	1	2	3	4	5
7. I don't lose emotional control or get overly distracted when I leave a spare that seems unfair—for example, a split or a single pin— when I thought I threw a good shot.	1	2	3	4	5
8. I keep my motivation and sense of purpose strong whether I am way ahead or way behind in the game or in the set.	1	2	3	4	5
9. I can stay totally focused on the present shot and game, no matter what occurred in previous shots or games. I can do this no matter what is at stake if I do well or poorly.	1	2	3	4	5
10. If I throw a bad shot—for example, chucking it into the channel or whiffing at a single-pin spare— I quickly pull myself together and focus on the here and now for my next shot.	1	2	3	4	5

is the same pattern the average person has for most behavior-change commitments. Just note the low success rate for weight-loss clinics, smoking-cessation programs, and exercise plans.

Excellent bowlers simply do what they say they will do. Their word really is their bond; they offer no excuses. How these special bowlers feel runs second to the commitment to follow through on practice and performance goals. Their two most important traits are their intention to excel in bowling and their sense of personal integrity in following through on their commitments. To join their ranks, you must be able to say truthfully, "I do what I say I will do," and mean it. This is where you truly get to find out if you are a person of your word.

The questionnaire in table 1.3 is designed to test your level of commitment. As in the previous self-assessment, be fully and completely honest with your answers. Assign a number from 1 to 5 to each statement. A 1 means the statement is least true for you; a 5 means it is most true.

Now add up your points. The score range is similar to that for mental strength. A total of 40 points or higher puts you up there with athletes who seek and find excellence. You are a likely candidate for having what it takes to deal with the training efforts and comfort zone stretches needed to take your mental game to higher levels.

If you scored below 40, analyze each statement to find out where your commitment strengths and weaknesses are. Each statement tells a story about what might be getting in the way of breaking out of your normal patterns of thinking, training, and competing. Look where you have a 3 or less and decide if this is an area that you care to address.

Once you have decided to take action, the options for interventions are numerous. The first option, of course, is to dig into this book and take on the exercises and ideas. You will find plenty in the following chapters to feed each of the identified issues in the survey. Other options include working with a coach or sport psychologist and reevaluating your goals in the sport.

TABLE 1.3   COMMITMENT QUESTIONNAIRE

Read the 10 statements and choose a number from 1 to 5 that most closely represents your own experience. A 1 means the statement is least true for you. A 5 means the statement is most true.

STATEMENT	FALSE				TRUE
1. I am willing to put aside other activities and miss social occasions and events in order to excel in bowling.	1	2	3	4	5
2. I greatly desire to become an outstanding bowler.	1	2	3	4	5
3. I will keep practicing, studying, competing—whatever it takes—to achieve my bowling goals.	1	2	3	4	5
4. I don't blame the lane conditions, other bowlers, or the ball for my mistakes or failures. I know that ultimately it always comes down to me.	1	2	3	4	5
5. No matter how I feel or how I am bowling, when I practice I always give it my very best effort.	1	2	3	4	5
6. No matter what the score is when I'm in a tournament, league, or match play, I always give my very best effort.	1	2	3	4	5
7. I exercise to stay in bowling shape, read bowling materials, get coaching, and think about aspects of my mental game when I'm not actually competing or practicing.	1	2	3	4	5
8. I keep practicing even when I am tired, bored, or don't otherwise feel like it (including when I have minor aches and pains).	1	2	3	4	5
9. I am as interested and invested in excelling in bowling as I am in just about anything else I do.	1	2	3	4	5
10. Bowling is a lot of fun and makes me feel happy. It is the area of my life in which I am recognized as being someone.	1	2	3	4	5

I often work with experienced amateurs and professionals who tell me they just feel burned out. Some have lost their enthusiasm for bowling. Others have lost hope that they will find the fire again or fear the disappointments of reaching for the golden ring again and falling short. In most such cases, the athlete can, with help, discover where exactly the air went out of the fun and excitement balloon, as well as what he or she has lost in terms of the meaning of participating in the sport.

As you work through this book, you can revisit these assessment surveys to keep tabs on your mental strength and commitment. You are going to need both to excel in this demanding sport. The great news is that if you really want Olympian focus, intensity, and competition steel, you can have it. You may or may not be good enough to beat the best in the world. You can, however, learn to match or best anyone's mental game.

Look at your scores from the mental strength self-evaluation questionnaire in table 1.2 and your score in the commitment questionnaire in table 1.3. Is one score significantly higher than the other? If your commitment score is low or lower than your mental strength score, you may experience the frustration of having goals that you don't have the commitment to make happen. People low on commitment have to rely completely on super talent or incredible luck. If your mental game is lacking but your commitment is high, you probably have had your share of frustration, but your commitment gives you a real shot at succeeding.

How to Get There

So where are you going? Minimum thought with maximum flow is where you are going. You are looking to develop the mental toughness that enables you to be totally focused, involved, and in command, throwing the ball with all of your skill in an effortless way. You don't guide or force your shot; you simply deliver in just the right way at the right time.

This is not a book about developing the physical game. This is a guide for allowing the physical game to unfold in the most natural and effective way. From this stance of mental resilience, you will

- adjust to changes in lane and bowling center conditions;
- deal effectively with the performance demands of competition;

- lock in on your preshot routine;
- use your own spare system reliably;
- zero in on your strike shot;
- keep your focus under all conditions;
- handle bowling burnout;
- communicate effectively with your teammates, coaches, and students; and
- have a completely toned mental game.

If this is your goal, then buckle up. You can go for the ride of your life!

chapter

2

ENVISIONING SUCCESS ON THE LANES

In the early 1960s President Kennedy informed the world that the United States was going to put a man on the moon. At the time, those involved in the space program did not yet have the know-how to get the job done. NASA was only a few years old!

What President Kennedy presented to the citizens of the United States was a compelling vision of where he intended to lead the nation. He offered an energizing invitation to the entire country to come with him, and he powerfully mobilized the resources required to get the job done. On July 16, 1969, President Kennedy's vision was realized. The Apollo 11 rocket blasted off for the moon. Four days later, Neil Armstrong took the first lunar stroll. President Kennedy had demonstrated a platinum model in vision, commitment, and ultimate achievement.

This chapter is designed to help you establish a vision of the bowler you intend to be. You will set your goals accordingly and then decide what kind of push you are going to put into play to become that bowler. This is your own mission to the bowling moon. To succeed, you will have to make an honest assessment of what is working and what is breaking down for you.

First, sit back and really think about where you are going with your bowling. No kidding, no pie-in-the-sky craziness, no taking it easy by lowering the high-jump bar to something you can already reach. Without a clear vision of where you intend to go with your bowling, you are in serious danger of not going anywhere. You go where your eyes are looking.

The three essential ingredients for vision success are a clear vision and definition of what you intend to do, self-credibility, and an action plan that will make your vision a reality. Wishing is never enough.

Let's consider these three ingredients in order. Reading books about the sport, playing on a league team, doing tournaments, and practicing at lunch may all help your game, but progress can often be sluggish or nonexistent. Most people practice when they feel like it and skip practice when they don't. They credit fortune if they have a high-scoring outing. If you ask typical, B-plus to A-minus competitive bowlers what they intend to be averaging, what skills they intend to improve, and even what they intend to do in tournaments, most have no real plan. However, talk to coaches of high-level bowlers (or elite athletes in any other sport, for that matter), and they will have a vision and a plan.

Vision and Mission

Before we continue, you should understand the difference between hope and real vision. A wise man once said that those who dine on hope soon starve to death. Hope is leaving it up to the bowling gods to make you strong and coordinated, to make sure the lanes are oiled right, and to have a messenger pin take out the 10-pin. Hope relies heavily on chance, luck, and fate.

Successful businesses have vision and mission statements that declare what the business stands for and provide stockholders with plans for how to achieve high financial goals. Successful athletes have their own versions of vision and mission statements. Vast amounts of research suggest that this is a good idea.

Vision is a portrait painted with words that states what you intend to accomplish. The mission part is a simple, brief description of what you are going to do to get there. The two kinds of visions are personal performance and competition outcome. You have a great deal of control over the achievement of personal performance goals. Competition outcome goals feed the ego, but are more difficult to predict. Fortunately, personal performance goals tend to lead to positive competition outcomes without your even having to tweak your game.

Personal performance goals focus on all the things you can do to improve your game independently of how anyone else bowls, goals such as raising your average, improving your percentage of solid pocket hits, improving spare shooting, strengthening your mental game, and so forth. Competition outcome goals are concerned with beating opponents and winning tournaments or championships.

There is a significant difference between personal performance goals and competition outcome goals. You can achieve a personal performance goal (PG) of throwing 12 pocket shots in a game, but still not have a perfect game. Likewise, you can bowl a great game with a solid base, good balance, great timing, and powerful delivery (all personal PGs); score a solid 260; and still be beat by someone else's 270 game.

Working on personal performance goals sets up higher scores, increases your chances of winning cash, and improves your chances at winning. Focusing on competition outcome goals may serve as motivation, but far too much is out of your control. The point is to become a great bowler, especially under pressure. That is all you have control over. Focus on that, and when it is your day to win, you will be ready to meet it.

Deciding on competition goals is like setting a point on a compass. You point your finger and say, "I am going there, no kidding!" Having a direction helps you set up a training and competition program. Your competition outcome goals also let your coach know how hard to push you. In addition, you can see which training behaviors are in line with where you declared you are going.

Personal performance goals give you a training focus. You know where you want to go, and you have a plan to get there.

If you decide that competition outcome goals are the most important (scores, titles, money, etc.), then you invite two major risks. First, your happiness and sense of satisfaction are tied to pin fall and pin carry, other bowlers' abilities and performances, and having your A game with you all the time. Second, you risk creating increased pressure and concern as you bowl. Ironically you can actually bowl worse as you raise the importance (in your mind) of having to put up a certain number, or even as you become aware that you are close to achieving your goals. Pressure can increase even more if you have not won for a while or if you came close to a championship but didn't win.

If you choose to focus on personal performance goals, you can have a positive and satisfying experience even if you leave a ringing 10-pin (in which the 10-pin stands even though a pin rings around it) or someone else bowls a better game. Performance goals focus on skill sets, such as being balanced at the line, having a free armswing, using proper thumb release timing, and hitting the mark a certain percentage of the time.

Perhaps the easiest, and ultimately most satisfying, performance goal to achieve is to bowl freely and wholeheartedly. This was referred to in chapter 1. To throw 6, 8, 12, or more shots a game with total commitment, heart, and effort will wring the maximum effect out of any physical game development you will ever have.

There are two important reasons for making personal performance goals your highest priority. First, you can measure self-improvement without relying on lane conditions, other bowlers, or pin fall. Second, a focus on personal performance goals gives you your best chance at winning and improving. Competition goals are fine for offering a compass point or direction, but counting them as a priority is less likely to advance your game or bring success.

Your Word

Before we get into the how-to, I have some questions for you. Are you a person of your word? Are you credible? Do you do what you say you are going to do? Do you trust yourself? What has your success rate been on keeping resolutions? How have you been at keeping promises to yourself?

Vision and goal setting without action is merely fantasy. You may say what you are going to do, what you intend to win or score, and how you will train, but if you are like the typical promise or resolution maker, you may well trip up in your follow-through. Here is an example. Let's say you make a New Year's resolution to run one mile on Mondays, Wednesdays, and Saturdays. For the first week, you execute perfectly. The weather is great. You feel strong and motivated. During the second week, things start to change. Your enthusiasm for the new program starts to wane. Your muscles complain a little bit. Then on Saturday the weather shifts. It is overcast, damp, and cool. You say to yourself, "I'm tired; the weather's no good. I think I'll wait until tomorrow."

When you change your plans without writing an escape clause into your personal resolution ahead of time, you have broken your word to yourself. If you are creative and inventive in justifying breaking your commitments, then envisioning and goal setting will have much less personal effectiveness. The solution is to hold yourself completely accountable for success or failure and for keeping your agreements.

Write It Down

Get a piece of paper and a pen. Better yet, start a bowling notebook. A notebook is great for recording goals, insights, league and tournament results, and trends, and for archiving league and tournament memorabilia. A well-kept notebook will become your own ready-access coach when your game breaks down and you need to review your bowling checkpoints.

Did you actually get a pen and journal? You can get a good look at your willingness to take action, and to be coached out of your comfort zone, simply by examining whether you are open to performing this one task.

Take a moment to write down your thoughts, feelings, and goals. What do you like best about bowling? Why are you so invested in the sport? Note your vision, dreams, and expectations for what you intend to accomplish. Do you love the challenge? Are you an athlete who has found a sport for your 30s, 40s, and beyond? Do you think you can run with the really big dogs? Do you want to learn to hook the ball a ton? Do you want to average 220 in league? Where are you going? List it all.

Don't set your sights too low. Low expectations will leave you bored with your goals and unsatisfied when you achieve them.

Set lofty but not crazy goals. Better to shoot for the moon and end up on a mountaintop than to shoot for something dinky and make no gains. However, if you set goals that are way out of your range, you risk becoming discouraged and giving up. Setting excessively high goals can be an easy excuse for not reaching any goals at all.

Be specific in your writing. Set up goals you can measure and evaluate in terms of successful bowling. Although performance goals should be your main focus, include competition outcome goals, too. Remember that as you meet performance goals, competition outcomes such as winning, cashing, and raising your average will improve as well.

Goals can be either short term or long term. Short-term goals can be defined as immediate or time-limited goals. Some examples of specific short-term goals are to have a strong balanced finishing position on every shot, to have repeatable correct thumb exit timing, to employ a reliable spare system, to hit the pocket on 90 percent of first shots, and to bring complete focus and attention to every shot in a game. Short-term goals can be integrated into your game in the long term. Once you attain them, they continue to serve you. They become basic parts of your repertoire that you can maintain, build on, and improve.

Long-term performance goals often take months or even years to achieve. Examples may include raising your average 20 or more points, making 95 percent of nonsplit spares consistently, mastering multiple hand positions, or earning a pro card. In addition to offering performance enhancement, long-term goals also often carry competition results, including titles, cash, making tournament cuts, and even hall of fame selections. As previously mentioned, these kinds of goals will steer training, coaching, and analysis of competition results. Use your notebook to record short-term and long-term goals. Your own experience and skill level will determine where you set your goals.

Evaluate Results

After a short period of time, you need to evaluate your goals and progress. It is important to accurately map out where you performed in terms of your stated goals. Skipping this step is a big mistake. That would be like an archer shooting arrows without ever bothering to look at the target.

Checking results equals poking your nose into the truth. If you can't handle feedback, you are in for a much longer, more painful road to improvement. To make the most of your short- and long-term goal evaluation, distinguish between taking stock of your improvement and taking stock of yourself. Bowling feedback is not about you personally. It is only about your bowling.

True feedback is difficult for many people. Think of the first time you heard your voice on audiotape (most of us think there is something wrong with the batteries) or saw yourself on videotape ("Whoa, that's what I look like from behind?!!"). It can be startling to view yourself from a neutral and objective standpoint. Many athletes tend to focus on the negatives of falling short of perfect goal attainment. This is a mistake. You must be willing to accept accurate feedback about movement and goal achievement while learning to remain positive, encouraged, and excited about your progress. Without the willingness to examine the truth about your form and your results, your progress will be much slower.

You can use any written form to declare what you will do. Just make sure that you have a way to keep yourself honest about follow-through. Post your goals where you can see them. Develop a user-friendly, reliable system for recording and tracking personal performance and competition outcome goals. Figure 2.1 shows a sample bowling achievement log, and figure 2.2 shows a sample bowling performance evaluation. These are examples only. Any particular goal or system that works for you is the system to use.

Name: Date:

Skill/activity	Strong	Average	Needs improve-ment	Specific goal	Target date
Spare shooting			X	Learn reliable spare system; make 80% of nonsplit spares	Nov. 11
Balance at the line		X		Show strong, stable finishing position on every shot	Oct. 15
Pocket hits		X		Learn to hit my mark and hit pocket on 90% of first shots	Dec. 1

Figure 2.1 Bowling achievement log.

Name: Event and date:

Skill/activity	Available statistics or personal/coach rating (1 to 100%)	Comments
Spare shooting	Made 16 of 20 nonsplit spares (80%)	Pulled head up early on missed spares
Balance at the line	Solid, no wobble on 30 of 36 shots (approximately 85%)	All six wobbles were on corner pin spares
Pocket hits	Hit the pocket on 22 of 33 first shots (66%)	Need to follow through on release

Figure 2.2 Bowling performance evaluation log.

An important move to make is to have a coach, teammate, or friend witness your goals. Something about making a public declaration inspires us to keep commitments. You can coach only athletes who are willing to put themselves at stake for what they say they want to do and learn. Telling someone what you plan to accomplish puts you and your word on the line.

Obviously there is no limit to the physical and mental game skills you could record in logs such as the examples in figures 2.1 and 2.2. Seeing the evidence of changes in your game gives you satisfaction as you master the game. Increased skill development is linked to increased self-confidence as well.

It is not enough to clarify specific goals. You must also have an action plan for getting there (Murphy 1996). Like everything else in goal setting, the action plan must be specific and measurable, which simply means that goals and changes are spelled out in such a way that you can say for sure whether you followed through. This is vital because compliance with your action plan will tell you what is working or what is not in your training program.

How well you follow through on the action plan demonstrates your degree of commitment, dedication, and stick-to-it-iveness. As a side note, most people notice that they have similar levels of commitment and word keeping in other parts of their lives as they do on their action plans. This is one aspect of sport that provides you with a chance to build character as well as skill. How you address your bowling commitments will likely mirror how you address other life commitments.

Your action plan is the "how much by when" part of the process. In the action plan, you lay out what it takes to have the results you say are important to you. You list the number of practice sessions, daily repetitions of single-pin spares, number of coaching contacts, and so on, that will take place. If you skip this step, you leave a bit more in the realm of luck than in the kingdom of "I did what I said I would do."

The three rules of action plans are to keep them simple, specific, and measurable. When the day, week, or tournament is over, you have to be able to look at your action plan and know, yes or no, whether you followed it. This step is vital because whether or not you follow through on the action plan will tell you about your own level of commitment as well as whether you have set up a good program.

Pick out a skill or activity. Lay out how to go about mastering it, follow your plan, and then take a look at what you accomplished. Table 2.1 illustrates a sample action plan.

As you can see, the action plan is really another way of declaring yourself. This is not about playing it safe. It is about putting yourself in gear and participating fully. Playing it safe is for people who only watch bowlers on television. You are placing yourself in the arena by committing to action.

TABLE 2.1 SAMPLE ACTION PLAN

Skill/activity	Action plan	Accomplishment record
Making 10-pin spares (90%)	Will practice three times a week for three weeks; shoot 20 10-pins per practice	Made 7 of my 9 commitments
Pocket hits	Will practice three times a week for three weeks (part of other practice sessions); count how many times out of 20 I hit my pocket shot mark	Made 7 of my 9 commitments

Review the completion of your action plan commitments. Remember these basics:

- Keep the action plan manageable. Don't overwhelm yourself with requirements.
- Keep the action plan consistent with your own level of interest. Practice skills that match your level of play as well as your hopes and dreams concerning where your game is going.
- Look at your accomplishments and struggles with a critical eye. Not achieving the desired result in terms of skills and scores is different from not keeping your word about training commitments. If you break your training schedule, consider the possibility that you set up something too hard or too boring to complete. Bowling doesn't just build character, it reflects character, too. Do you break or keep your word elsewhere? The answer is probably the same.

Figure 2.3 is a sample journal page that you can copy and use to record your own personal vision for success.

Potholes and Pitfalls

Let's look at some of the most common pitfalls in setting and completing goals. Watch out for these. Just like encountering a pothole in the road, you can hit one of these problems before you know it and significantly damage your plans to become a better bowler.

To have the best results with your vision, mission, and action plans, watch out for the following:

- *Goal blizzard.* This is the practice of setting so many goals that you lose focus, can't adequately monitor how you are doing on each of your goals, and perhaps end up getting bored or overwhelmed by record keeping. Maybe later, when you get good at the goal setting and action-plan process, you can increase the number of goals in your personal plan. For starters, keep the number of short-term goals at around three. Rank them in order of importance.

Name: Date:

Short-term bowling goals:

1.

2.

3.

Long-term bowling goals:

1.

2.

3.

Specific skill/activity	Self-rating (1 to 10)	Specific goals	Target date

Performance evaluation

Specific event and date:

Skill/activity	Personal record/how I did (1 to 100%)	Comments
Goal 1		
Goal 2		
Goal 3		

Action plan

Skill/activity	Action plan (what you will do by when)	Accomplishment review
Goal 1		
Goal 2		
Goal 3		

Figure 2.3   Bowling goal achievement journal.

- *Goal mush.* This means setting goals that look good but are too general to measure. For example, improving the first shot, getting better at spares, and improving the mental game are fine targets, but you must have a measurable way of knowing you are improving. If you want to clean up these goals, for example, you could modify them to improving first-shot pocket hits from the current average of 7 per game to 10, increasing your spare-making percentage from 75 to 85 percent, or practicing any of the mental game tools from this book a declared percentage of shots per game.

- *Goal fit.* The goals you set must have some juice for you. If you are going after something that fits a coach's needs or something that you think you are supposed to do but don't really desire, you are set up to ultimately fail in complying with your own program. If the action plan is too easy or too demanding, you will probably wash out. Set goals that fit your style, personality, and life.

- *Goal lock.* Goal lock happens when you fail to change and modify goals based on performance. Throughout practices and competitions, you will see which goals are too far reaching, or too simple, at any given time. If you fail to reset your sights, you will sabotage your goal-setting program. If you are not achieving your goals, simply readjust desired improvements into smaller bites. This is not failure. It is being smart about your growth as an athlete.

- *Outcome goal tunnel vision.* Remember that outcome goals (scores, victories, and money) depend on external factors such as pin fall and the performances of competitors. Tying your sense of success or failure solely to winning, particularly in any one tournament, is a setup for frustration, low self-esteem, and quitting. Performance goals that have to do with personal improvement in skill areas and execution will leave you feeling satisfied, believing in your bowling, and eager to set new challenging goals. (Again, you also are more likely to have positive competition results.)

Tying goals to external factors such as pin fall may lead to frustration. Set goals based on performance improvements and let the pins fall as they may.

Breakdown

The final aspect of your personal vision for success is knowing how to deal with both falling short of declared goals and action plans and achieving your intended results. The Japanese have a process called *kaizan*, which means continual improvement and a search for excellence. Look at what you achieved, where you are succeeding in the overall game of improvement, and where you have stumbled as well. Follow this essential step early and often.

The excellence protocol has five steps:

1. Look at and acknowledge goals you met and didn't meet and plans you followed and didn't follow. This can be a bit challenging to begin with. Some people have a hard time recognizing what they have done well, particularly if they have made declarations to others. At the same time, most of us do not like to look at our own shortcomings. (It's like seeing a pimple on your face. You look at another place in the mirror.) Tell the truth. You might or might not like what you see, but you will know what to do next.

2. Immediately review the parts of the plan that assisted you in being successful. This will get your feedback and examination off on the right foot. You also want to make sure when recalibrating new goals that you don't throw the baby out with the bathwater, meaning that you discard things that are working. Simply start by asking, what worked? No matter what happened, if you clear your head, you can always find positive aspects of your bowling.

3. Figure out why you did not complete any unfulfilled goals. Don't jump on your own case. Stay away from judging yourself. If you have a shame attack, you are going about this incorrectly. Look at your motivation, some of the pitfalls and potholes discussed earlier, and other unforeseen problems.

4. Think about what you have to modify or change to meet your training and competition goals. You can clarify your action plan, hire a coach, mark out training time in your calendar, or whatever might be called for to make necessary changes. List the answer.

5. Modify your commitments, goals, and action plans, and go forth. Be bold. Shoot for the moon. Just make sure you can make it for the launch (develop a good training plan) to achieve a lunar

landing. And once again, make sure you spell your action plans out in ways that you can examine and measure later.

Go through this excellence process early and often. As time goes on, it will become second nature to you and you will be able to complete the five steps rapidly. Once you start holding yourself accountable for what you achieve, or don't achieve, you give up blaming and feeling helpless and get to experience the power of goal setting, commitment, and success that true champions experience.

In a nutshell, you are simply declaring your intention to do something important and your plans for accomplishing it. Once you have taken action, look at what you actually did. Decide if you kept your word about the actions you would take and if you got the results you were shooting for. Then, whether your answer is yes or no, set your sights anew for what you will do next.

One final note: Envisioning is a constant updating and reviewing process. As you become more masterful with your bowling, you will find yourself clarifying your next steps in tight, measurable, meaningful terms. Don't wait too long to review and revise. The sky is the limit. Go see.

chapter

3

ESTABLISHING A PRESHOT ROUTINE

Elite golfers, gymnasts, divers, and bowlers all have to execute key skills at critical moments, and they have to do it alone; no one is allowed to touch the athlete or change the game. The performer is simply called on to deliver the goods in front of the entire universe. This leaves all kinds of time for mental gears to churn in preparation.

World-class athletes who have to execute on their own without facing a defense often have developed preskill routines that help them clear their minds and shake off pressure. For instance, Michael Jordan has a set number of bounces and spins with the basketball before shooting a free throw. Tiger Woods lines up his shot, measures his swing, sets his feet, and then swings. Baseball pitchers handle rosin bags, spit, rub the ball, and then throw. Great athletes from every sport, including professional bowlers, know to set themselves up to repeat desired action sequences.

What no one can see is the silent part of a great athlete's preshot routine. That part is every bit as essential as going through the physical motions. The goal of the preshot routine is to firmly establish the three Cs—concentration, confidence, and control—by combining physical behaviors with mental preparation.

The preshot routine is a standard, established sequence of thoughts and motions that the bowler performs before rolling the ball in game situations. Preshot sequences serve to focus, coordinate, and relax the bowler, increasing the probability of throwing a great shot. Although the physical part of the preshot routine is obvious, there are treasures to be found in the silent mental part of a great athlete's preshot routine. Internal preshot self-direction is every bit as essential as the physical sequence. In reality the mental and physical aspects of the preshot routine are so intertwined that it would take surgical intervention to separate them. Attending to one without the other keeps the athlete from reaching maximum potential.

Top bowlers go through set sequences of behaviors before they roll their shots, regardless of the situation, tournament or practice. Sometimes the preshot routine starts all the way back when the bowler rises out of the chair; sometimes the bowler pulls the act together just before going to the line by wiping the ball off, drying hands, or shuffling feet.

Competition environments are complex. They contain two environments, actually: the external environment and the one inside the bowler's head. Random and unsettling events can occur in both. Lane conditions, other competitors jumping up out of turn, noise, lights, and an unfamiliar lane away from the home center are examples of factors in the external environment. The internal environment includes questions about great shots and errant shots, ball choices, and the importance of the next rolled ball. Get a hundred bowlers in a room and you will hear a hundred or more stories about the crazy and distracting thoughts that go shooting through their minds in high-intensity situations.

The preshot routine is a way to create order out of chaos. It is a way to set the gears of a complex machine so they run smoothly under any circumstances. In this chapter we will explore some very good psychological reasons for making sure you have a consistent, rehearsed preshot routine.

Courtesy of Dean Hinitz

The preshot routine helps a bowler minimize the distractions in the external bowling environment.

Prediction and Control in High-Intensity Settings

A basic psychological survival principle seems to support the good sense of developing a preshot routine. This principle centers on prediction and control. To suspend anxiety and have confidence, a person needs to have a sense of prediction concerning what is going to happen and control over his or her effective responses to the situation.

This makes perfect sense in survival terms. Think about life before the safety of towns and cities. People living in the wild had to be able to notice changes in the environment rapidly and predict the behaviors of other creatures such as saber-toothed tigers or human enemies. If they could not predict what was going to happen, or take control over their fight-or-flight options, primitive men and women were likely to end up as some hungry animal's lunch or get caught in a raging storm. Prediction gave them time to prepare; control over responses gave them the opportunity to avoid the situation or prevent it from escalating to a dangerous point.

Anxiety leads to vigilance, which, in the case of primitive people, was probably a good thing. Without the ability to predict when trouble would strike, or a sense of control over some situations, however, primitive people would have been anxious all the time. When anxiety becomes overwhelming, it leads to panic, which severely diminishes fine motor coordination. Cave people learned to attend to signs and signals that something was going to happen, which helped them handle danger. But they also had to be able to control their anxiety to keep it from turning into panic.

Interestingly, this has direct application to the bowling center. The wild atmosphere of the bowling center can be thought of as all of the unpredictable thoughts, feelings, noises, lighting, and lane conditions that might attack concentration, attention, and confidence. The internal sense of danger can come from pressured thoughts of having to win or having a bad outcome. Your task is to introduce order, control, and predictability into the competitive situation. The preshot routine allows you to establish a sense of steadiness and safety in the face of all the possible internal and external distractions and threats you may experience.

Ultimately, you should strive to achieve the ideal performance state whenever you compete. The goal is to take the best of what you achieved in practice, when your mental and emotional state is relaxed and unpressured, and translate it into league and tournament play. To do this, you need to groove in the preshot routine in practice, when bowling is free flowing and your mental state is unharried. The preshot routine will then become a natural part of competition bowling, signaling to the unconscious mind that everything is in good hands and under control. This routine will also prepare you to go through the entire shot cycle described in chapter 4.

Setting Up an Effective Preshot Routine

The preshot routine is created by establishing a chain of naturally related events. This creates a sense of order. It is human nature to have events that happen in sequence cue the same sequence to repeat over and over again. The chain of events can be created consciously or unconsciously.

For example, smokers who like to smoke after meals automatically have thoughts and reactions that cue them to want to smoke after they eat. People who like to snack when they read or watch television start getting munchie urges when they pull out a book or turn on the television. Smoking is like a preshot routine for winding down after a meal. Eating is like a preshot routine for relaxed reading or television viewing.

The natural human tendency is to automatically associate pleasant and positive events with the thoughts, feelings, and actions that precede them. By actively designing the links in the brain before bowling, you make use of this tendency. Planning and organizing a preshot sequence will help you attain better performances, such as those found in practice, all the time.

The obvious place to start in designing a preshot routine is with motions you already use before you roll the ball. The great majority of experienced bowlers already have characteristic habitual patterns. Some behaviors are easily recognized; some are not. The task is to pick three to five elements of the approach sequence that lead to shot delivery. Then, use these same elements every time you prepare to roll a ball as a way of cueing attention, focus, and positive feelings.

Setting up the preshot routine is like throwing a lasso around concentration. Though you can't expect to keep all thoughts from your mind, you can learn to keep your mind from wandering so

A consistent preshot routine creates a feeling of order as you prepare to make the shot.

much that your concentration shifts. A personalized routine pattern steers concentration in a single direction even when other thoughts and noises intrude.

Designing the Preshot Routine

The first part of preshot design is observation. You already have three to five behaviors that are characteristic of your approach. Look for actions that provide a feeling of being synchronized, like in this example:

> I take a full relaxing breath, inhale and exhale, at the ball return. I wipe off the ball. I take a good look at the lines and visualize the mark and projected ball path. I silently say the word *trust* in my mind. As I do, I feel the surge of trust in my ability and training and the ball's design to roll properly. I set my feet. I see the mark one more time. Then I roll the ball.

Everyone has a personal sequence. Make sure your preshot routine has these four essential elements (Vernaccia, McGuire, and Cook 1996):

1. *Observation and awareness.* Observe the lanes and surrounding competition area. Note anything that is important to be aware of: pin configuration on spares, oil-pattern mapping, sources of noise, and so on. You have nothing else to do at this point except conduct a comprehensive scan. Remember prediction and control? Awareness of the playing field lends a sense of mastery to being in the bowling competition environment. You can't, of course, control everything. Lane oil is invisible, bad racks can be hard to spot, and other people behave unpredictably. Decide what is important for you to notice and take into account and let the rest go. Having your own preshot plan and ritual will give you an essential sense of control over what you can do, no matter what is happening around you.

2. *Strategy.* Have a strategy for where to focus attention. A hundred things could distract you, including various thoughts, emotions, physical sensations, noises, and other bowlers. No matter what else is knocking on the doors and windows of your awareness, the preshot routine provides a place to focus attention. Some common points of focus are having a relaxed armswing,

keeping a steady head, watching the mark, and being solid at the line. Other possibilities include generating warm confidence, using positive self-talk about what you will do, and imagining putting energy into the ball. Pick what works for you and employ it consistently until it becomes as much a part of you as physical muscle memory.

3. *Visualization.* Visualize what the ball will do on the lane. Points of intention include roll and rotation, ball path, and breakpoint. Seeing the ball behavior, as if viewing the future, can result in your mind and body's making all kinds of subtle adjustments to create the visualization intention. When visualizing, you should be mentally, physically, and emotionally in the moment of what you are about to create. If you have the bowling skills to make it happen, your unconscious mind can powerfully fulfill your visualized intention. An important note here is that great visualizers focus only on what they intend their body and ball to do. They stay away from thinking about the consequences of making or missing the shot.

4. *Cues.* Have a cue thought or word. Having a cue word is like pulling on one strand of a spider web and having all the strands come together in a collapsing net. All mental, emotional, and physical training can mesh smoothly together without having to think about it. In the earlier example, the bowler used the word *trust.* Other useful cue words for bowlers are *pose* for finishing in a balanced bowling-trophy position, and *smooth* or *energy.* Some bowlers prefer to have cue phrases such as *Be an athlete, I am strong,* or *I am solid.* The point is to have a silent verbal signal that coordinates and focuses you. It is best to keep it brief.

The preshot routine is one of the most reliable tools in the mental game arsenal. It sets up a sequence of positive thoughts, feelings, and actions. It is easy to take with you into any location or situation. Additionally, it is an internal resource that generates familiarity, positive feelings, and a sense of control over your own reactions in pressured competition situations.

The Three Cs

Championship bowlers demonstrate the three Cs of champions: consistency, confidence, and control. Clearly, the preshot routine is an effective setup for all three. Given that a bowler rolls hundreds, sometimes thousands, of shots during a tournament, the ability to repeat good shots is essential. Knowing that you have a means of focusing coordination and attention boosts your sense of confidence. Owning and practicing your preshot routine effectively can lead to a wonderful sense of overall control of the game.

To have the benefits of consistency, confidence, and control, you must practice your preshot routine consistently in training. Don't ever roll a throwaway shot, not during training, not during league play, not during tournaments. Every shot is an opportunity to redefine, regroove, and rehearse the preshot routine. Don't skip this step in bowling even when you are horsing around, blowing through a few frames, or just warming up. Lock it in. Following this practice will help you build trust in yourself so you won't have to be concerned about distractions and changes in the competition environment.

All bowlers seek a sense of prediction and control over shots, games, attention, and confidence. The preshot routine is an internal message system that tells the brain "Ground control to competition brain, now starting the system sequence to liftoff." Go through these four stages:

1. See the lanes and pin configuration (on spares). Have a clear picture of the field of play.
2. Pick your strategy. Know the ball, the line the ball should follow, and perhaps ball rotation and breakpoint, if these more technical aspects are part of your game.
3. Engage the rest of the preshot sequence that gets you onto the approach and prepared to roll. List three to five essential elements of your preshot routine and keep the list in your bowling log.
4. Say the cue word you selected and practiced. Then go for it.

These steps can be employed in any order. Add, subtract, mix, or match them in the way that works best for you. Don't worry about taking the extra few seconds you might need to own an effective internal rhythm. Every bowler has to get to the ball, view the lanes, breathe, and deliver the ball anyway.

In chapter 4 you will learn to integrate the preshot routine into the overall repeating cycle of shots. With the proper mental mind-set, you can make every bowling center feel like your home center.

chapter

STAYING IN SYNC THROUGH THE SHOT CYCLE

One of the frustrations of bowlers at every skill level, from beginner to touring professional, is the change in tension levels, feel for the ball, and timing when entering a competitive situation. Bowlers who deliver the ball wonderfully in practice, even shadow practice right before the competition, sometimes lose their coordination and steadiness when the lights come on.

Many great bowlers exhibit deliveries and shot cycles that are beautifully synchronized, or in sync. To be in sync means to be in the right frame of mind and to be physically coordinated from the time the ball is picked up, through the delivery and release, and into the recovery and preparation phase for the next shot. Hall of famers Dick Weber and Earl Anthony, 2002 U.S. Open winner Kim Terrell, and 2002 Bowler of the Year Carolyn Dorin-Ballard are all examples of bowlers who have marvelously synchronized shot cycles.

I suppose it would be bad manners to identify professionals who have fragmented or unbalanced shot cycles. Most of us can recognize when an athlete appears to be overly mechanical when the pressure is on, or overcome with anger or frustration when things are going badly. Bowlers who don't regroup after an errant shot of their own, or a great clutch shot by an opponent, show up for ensuing shots looking rushed or frazzled. This often results in a continued decline in performance for the remainder of the game.

There are many ways to regulate the competition engine so that shots can be executed as cleanly and confidently as in practice. One of the best is to have a sense of control over the accelerator and the brake in the internal nervous system. When people talk about someone getting nervous, it simply means that action hormones like adrenaline are sending messages throughout the body. The energy conductors, the nerves in the body, become overly agitated. In this chapter you will learn to set up and manage your thoughts and feelings from beginning to end for superior shots and games under any circumstances.

If your only exposure to competitive bowling was watching professional bowlers on television, you could easily have the illusion that top athletes simply do not get tense, anxious, or worried about performance. Many of the top pros seem calm and cool as they deliver shot after shot. During the 2002 PBA World Championships, for instance, the number one seed Brian Voss never missed a single-pin spare all week. However, every now and then we see a pro get fast on the delivery or miss a single-pin spare. For example, Lonnie Waliczek bowled against Voss in the semifinal on television. Waliczek followed a four-strike string with a missed four-pin spare. (Waliczek held on to win the match). In the other semifinal, Doug Kent was bowling against Rick Steel-smith. Kent followed a three-bagger with a missed 10-pin spare that nearly cost him the match. (Kent strung enough strikes to cover the mistake and ultimately win the competition.) Let's consider some of the reasons this might happen.

Many bowlers, even elite, professional bowlers, can worry about doing well and overactivate their nerves, making their hands sweaty and their coordination jerky and causing them to lose their appetites. Overthinking takes on a life of its own. Other bowlers manage to remain in sync despite feelings of excitement and nervous tension. The difference is that they have learned to tame anxiety to bring out the best in high-stakes situations.

Staying in sync is about working effectively with excitement levels to call forth great performances under pressure. There is nothing wrong with emotional activation. This is the most normal thing in the world when participating in something important. In fact, the body does not make a distinction between the adrenaline surges created by fear, anxiety, or excited anticipation. It is up to you to harness the body's reactions productively.

Recognition

The first step in learning to stay in sync is to know when your emotional levels are interfering with your bowling. This can be difficult in the macho world of competitive athletics. Sometimes acknowledging basic human reactions to the excitement, concerns, hurts, and hopes of high-stakes league and tournament play can seem embarrassing. Athletes sometimes like to pretend that they do not experience the distracting, sometimes disturbing, feelings that everyone feels at times.

Any kind of game situation—from league play, to high-roller big cash prize tournaments, to trying to make the cut on the professional tour—can stimulate a range of feelings from excitement to overjuicing. Tension tends to escalate during specific moments in a game, such as when you have to make a key spare, when

© Sleeping Dogs Communications

The key to staying in sync is not to eliminate emotional play. The key is to control excitement so it enhances the competition without interfering.

you are finishing a game or series that is going very well (or very poorly), and when you are performing for an audience, either live or via television.

Ups and downs in performance reflect your skill and training. Bowling significantly or consistently worse in competition than in practice is a sure sign that your mental and emotional states are changing the way you deliver the ball.

At this point, a reminder is in order. Excitement and arousal are not emotional villains. A certain amount of excitement is helpful in getting us motivated. Having the juices flowing can also motivate increased focus and contribute to the true sense of fun that should be part of any competition. Every bowler has an optimum level of excitement at which he or she feels sufficiently motivated but not overwhelmed. When the emotional energy to compete is lacking, flatness, loss of focus, and boredom with the game can result. When the energy level is too high, choking can occur. Freedom of movement and flow can falter, coordination can get mechanical, and concerns and worries may increase.

Young and inexperienced bowlers may not even recognize what is happening to their emotions and energy. They may see that something is happening in terms of energy, tension, or distraction, but not know what it is, why it is occurring, or whether it is OK to talk about. No one wants to seem like a wimp. This keeps many bowlers from figuring out why they are feeling the way they do, and from getting appropriate assistance, support, or guidance.

Any competition-related feelings that come up are absolutely normal. Some of the most common are excitement, fear, nervousness, and anticipation. Just knowing that can relieve some bowlers of the worry that their particular reactions may not be normal. The trick to staying in sync, though, is being able to control your energy and excitement levels to optimize your performance. Simply having a plan for how to handle competition excitement is, in itself, stress relieving. The following sections offer some user-friendly techniques for dialing in the right energy and excitement levels.

Find the Tiger

Excitement, anxiety, and tension can show up in a variety of ways. At the most basic level, when a bowler begins to emotionally amp up in a competition situation, the mind and body are reacting as if risk or danger is present.

Fifty thousand years ago, humans played a different competitive game called survival. Imagine life as it was then. The competition arena was virtually everywhere. The game lasted as long as one could survive. Sometimes the threat was immediate—the growl of a tiger or a stranger with a club.

Back then, as now, when a critical moment appeared, the body went into a fight-or-flight response, causing blood to rush from the fingers, toes, and stomach to the big arm and leg muscles to prepare for action. Action-oriented hormones flushed through the bloodstream. Digestion stopped. Breathing became rapid and shallow. Fine-muscle coordination skills were sacrificed for large-muscle actions such as killing the tiger or climbing a tree. In your case, the pending action might be throwing a 15-pound ball for $100,000 or marking for a league championship.

The good news is that about three minutes after the event or threat passes, the body starts to go back to normal functioning. Blood flow returns to the fingers and toes. Fine-muscle coordination returns. Digestion and other metabolic processes flow efficiently again. The game is over. In the wild, the score is humans one, tigers zero.

When anxiety, overexcitement, concern, or fear become part of your bowling experience, your body begins to do the same things that it would do in a wilderness survival game. The mind and body activate into the fight-or-flight state in response to your emotional state. For example, you may want to win so badly that you can't sit still, or your fear of losing may speed up your heart rate. The reaction in your nervous system is similar to the one that would occur if a tiger growled in the bush. A problem occurs when you don't take the danger signals (for example, negative mental self-talk) out of the excitement response and do not allow for adequate, full recovery and clearing from excitement.

Three Keys to Managing Excitement

There are three keys to managing excitement in bowling competition situations. The first is to simply recognize the thoughts, feelings, and physical reactions that are happening. Young and inexperienced bowlers do not always have a name for the excitement that comes with performance demands. Other bowlers may feel general anxiety, but may be unsure of why it is happening. Worse yet is when athletes catastrophize, or worry that nervousness will run out of control. This puts even more pressure on their bowling.

The second key to managing excitement is to accept competition reactions without negative judgment. Some bowlers get embarrassed or even ashamed that they have excitement and tension reactions. Some degree of body response should be expected when bowling in an important game or tournament. Common body reactions include a queasy stomach, feeling hot or cold, having difficulty taking full breaths, dizziness, and overly mechanical motions when trying to coordinate shots.

The third key to managing excitement is to have a grab bag of techniques. Excitement management skills are like any other sport skill. They must be practiced regularly to make them a useful part of competition. Instead of toning up muscles, you are developing your mental and emotional thermostats. This will give you the confidence to know that you can handle any competition situation.

Mastering the Competition Cycle

Of all the focus and regulation techniques, having an ironclad plan for how to approach shots under any circumstances may be one of the all-time keys to the competition universe. Great bowlers know the secret by intuition. Bowlers who habitually fail often trip over the mystery. It is a tool that, once mastered, will deepen the well of confidence within you. This rare, desired competition treasure, which I call the *competition cycle*, will carry you through the toughest times once you master it.

Each shot, game, block, and tournament is part of a cycle of experience called the competition cycle. The competition cycle can be broken down into several stages or steps. Once you learn how the competition cycle works, you will be able to recognize some of the strengths and weaknesses in your mental game, but there are pitfalls if you over- or underemphasize a single part of the cycle.

The cycle has four phases: planning and intention, execution and commitment, reaction and emotion, and clearing and recovery. In this section, the stages of the competition cycle will be applied specifically to shot making, but the formula, once learned, can be expanded to larger aspects of the game of bowling, and the game of life, for that matter.

Remember these four phases. First, think about what you learned from the last shot or in warm-ups. Somewhere in your preshot routine, decide on your plan of action, what you intend to do, and how you intend to do it. Include a heart commitment. Second, bowl wholeheartedly as you turn your intention into movement. This is the time to profoundly trust your training and ability. Go for everything you intended in the planning phase. Third, allow yourself to react. You do not have to put on a show; just be real with yourself. You can learn a lot about heart and performance in this phase. Don't miss it. Also don't miss the joy of great execution. It will further groove your athletic memory for shot repetition. Finally, clear and recover. Get over your feelings, unless you are using them to help you in some way. Exhale. Clear your head. Rest for a moment. Then, when it's show time, begin the sequence again.

I can't imagine a sport, job, or important relationship that wouldn't have all of the same requirements in some way. Remember that this formula works for entire league and tournament outings, as well as for individual shot sequences. Master the competition cycle, and you will have complete confidence in your ability to bring great game anywhere, to any tournament, at any time.

I would like to thank Rick Benoit for his contributions in refining the competition formula.

Planning is over once you begin the approach. Execution and commitment are what matter now.

Planning and Intention

Phase 1 is planning and intention. You can start this phase as early as you like. As you prepare for your next shot, you should have some idea of what you intend to do. Planning and intention should be part of your preshot routine. On the approach, you make decisions about ball path, rotation, and ball speed, but you also have the opportunity to make decisions about how much you want to go for it, how free and athletic you want to be, and how much you are going to commit to your shot delivery.

The planning and intention phase is your chance to commit to the best you can bring. Use your history, coaching, and experience—all your acquired wisdom—to make decisions. At this point you get to pick whether to be a lion or a mouse. (A small competition tip—choose lion; you'll bowl better.)

Two common mistakes made in the planning and intention phase are too much or too little. In the planning phase, too little attention means inadequate preparation for the shot. This can result in sloppy shots, misplaying the lane, poor timing, inconsistent ball speed, and more. Inadequate planning means you won't have a clear idea of the level of dedication you want to bring to the shot and the game. Remember, lion or mouse; you have to choose every time.

Another common mistake in this phase is to overlap planning into the execution phase. Often bowlers continue to think about how to bowl or the consequences of making or missing the shot as they move forward into the delivery sequence. This results in overly careful, mechanical bowling. This is a prime setup for choking. When you decide to go, you must have nothing but "go" in you.

Execution and Commitment

Phase 2 is execution and commitment. Once you engage the motor gears, planning is over. In this phase, you let training take over. This step reflects complete and total surrender to what you intended in the planning phase. Remove the thoughts of consequences, old shots, outcomes, and even the audience. This step is about keeping a promise and demonstrating the total mental and physical commitment you made to yourself. The lion is committed. The mouse is always thinking and questioning.

In this phase, you may have one or two points of physical focus, such as balance, free armswing, eyes on the mark, or any other element you need to focus on. These points of focus serve to keep the whole mechanism coordinated. You need to do a heart check here as well. You either will bring it all or you won't. As you move through this step, the proof of your commitment

Don't let concerns about the score derail your shot cycle. Execute with full commitment to the shot.

should be obvious. You will know immediately after the delivery if you gave your all. Ball roll and pin fall likely will reveal your commitment level.

The biggest problem bowlers encounter in the execution phase is a failure to surrender completely to the shot. Whether they distrust the plan or distrust their own ability to perform, bowlers frequently are infected with the carefulness virus. Overcontrol and concern about results or the score get in the way of fully and freely delivering the shot.

In this phase, you must really let go of conscious control. This will make you truly athletic. You have a plan; go with it completely. If you do not compete with total commitment, success will feel like a trick. Failure will make you angry with yourself for holding back. I believe that most bowlers lose more sleep about not bringing all the athletic expression they trained for than they do about whether they marked.

Reaction and Emotion

Phase 3 is the reaction and emotion phase. Something significant has happened. You rolled a strike, made the spare, or missed. Unless you are made of stone, you will have some mental or emotional response to what has occurred. Your reaction may be subtle or intense, pleasant or noxious.

There is no correct emotional response. However you respond, though, you have a choice to acknowledge your reaction or stuff it down. Your mental and emotional response provides information to your conscious and unconscious mind; it also provides motivation in the form of positive feelings for successful completion of the execution and commitment phase.

After the shot, note how it felt, physically and emotionally, after you delivered it. If you can be completely honest with yourself, this instant feedback will help you know whether you brought all you had to the shot.

This phase has three primary risks: forbidding yourself to have any reaction, overreacting, and making rules about what you can and cannot allow yourself to feel. Some athletes and coaches believe you should behave like the Russian gymnasts from the 1960s: stoic, serious, and unfeeling. Generally this is an unnatural way to react. Whether you throw a great shot, carry a backdoor strike, or chop a spare, you are going to have some reaction.

Your emotional reaction to the shot will provide instant feedback. Did you bring everything you had?

Inhibiting reactions is like swallowing food in a balloon. You have it inside you, but you can't digest or metabolize it. Allow yourself the truth of your own reaction, exhale it, and move on. By the way, there are no good or bad feelings. Depending on how you rolled and the pin fall, you are likely to experience a range of reactions. This does not mean you have to act like a showman or a robot after the shot. This is not a demonstration for anyone else.

The alternative to having feelings is to be dead inside. Life without feelings is flat. Having a child, going to Disneyland, and throwing your first 300 game are all flat without some emotional life inside. Take charge, experience your experience, then move on.

Sometimes emotions and reactions can rule you. There is a time for all things, including moving to the next phase of clearing and recovery. Lingering in strong emotions for too long is a luxury that can cripple the entire shot cycle. Getting lost in anger and irritation will steer you past some of the learning and planning that are part of cleaning up any game. Basking in the glow of a great shot also can keep you from staying present with planning and execution. Have your reaction, digest it, and move on.

Clearing and Recovery

Everything in nature requires some form of recovery from mental and physical exertion to heal, reload, and prepare for what is to come. Training and competition are no exception. Phase 4 is the clearing and recovery phase. In this step you follow the laws of nature that demand rest and recovery before you can gear up for another maximum effort. This is the time to cut off your emotions and reactions from phase 3. You may decide to hang on to some aspect of the previous phase to learn from the last shot, then shake off any lingering emotional residue and catch a moment of rest. No matter what has happened, say to yourself, "That's what. So what. Now what?"

This step is the equivalent of a weightlifter's letting go of the bar completely before preparing for the next set, or a golfer's taking a mental break while walking to the green. Although the golfer must be aware of what happened to the ball, he or she can exhale after the shot to finish the reaction phase, start walking, then gear up into the planning phase again. Divers, archers, gymnasts, and baseball pitchers may go through a similar sequence to let go of whatever just happened and refocus on what is coming next. Any successful athlete who must execute an offensive sequence without confronting a defensive player can experience this cycle.

The classic abuse of the recovery phase occurs most often in training. Bowlers practicing alone risk overlapping one shot into the next as they grab balls off the ball return and prepare to fire the next shot. In league and tournament play, competitors get lost thinking about the last shot or immediately become concerned about the next shot. This pattern causes a constant drain on mental energy. To be successful you must clear the shot to have a fresh experience the next time up, even in training. If you get used to doing it in practice, you'll be more prepared to use it in competition.

Another trap in the clearing and recovery phase is mentally going so far away that you get lazy about refocusing and bringing energy back to the planning and intention part of the cycle. Mental clearing need not take more than a few seconds. Grab some water, talk to a teammate or coach, breathe and rest, whatever works for you. Just make sure to gear up when it's time to turn the ignition key again.

Brett Wolfe, winner of the 2002 ABC Masters, PWBA Bowler of the Nineties Wendy MacPherson, and former PBA Bowler of the Year Norm Duke are all recent examples of athletes who appeared to put the competition cycle to work. Even through the lens of a television camera, you could see these champions demonstrate the four phases throughout their games.

Excitement-Regulation Techniques

A variety of techniques exist to regulate excitement and relaxation. The keys to good tension thermostat control can be initiated either through the body systems or through the thought system. The techniques that follow are the real how-tos a professional bowler would learn from a sport psychologist.

The following sections offer several techniques. The way to decide which one to use is simple: Pick the one that works. Bowlers feel more or less comfortable with different mental and physical synchronization techniques. Some bowlers are good visualizers but are not good at self-talk. Some techniques are easy to use anywhere. Some may be difficult to employ without help from a coach or partner or a quiet place in which to use them. Bowlers may find some techniques natural, others awkward or odd. Use the ones that seem the most user-friendly to you, but make sure to try them all to discover what is going to work.

Breathing Skills

Within the shot cycle are opportunities to practice a wide variety of mental and emotional regulation skills. Probably the simplest of all body relaxation techniques is breathing awareness. Controlled breathing is especially useful if a bowler is plagued with distracting or disturbing thoughts—such as preoccupation with aspects of the game, the shot, or the release—in the heat of competition. The great thing about working with breathing skills is that everyone has to breathe anyway. You already have a lifetime of practice at it, and it doesn't take any extra time.

The first thing to do is simply to focus on the rhythm of breathing without changing anything. Merely notice the pace of inhalations and exhalations. Just turning attention to breathing for a moment can help you ease tension, but there is more to breath work than that.

If you are anxious, frustrated, or excited, chances are that your body is tight and your breathing is not really calming and relaxing. Remember the wild tiger in the example of the caveman. When the personal tiger growls at the outset of competition, you may find yourself taking quick, shallow breaths or even holding your breath altogether. Ironically, during a high-stakes bowling tournament, you must do just the opposite.

Shallow breathing brought on by an action fight-or-flight response creates muscle tension. It also sends a message to the unconscious self. The brain picks up on rapid, shallow breathing and sends a warning message to the whole body. This is not a helpful message, especially when you are dealing with anticipation and excitement, not danger. Such a message to the brain can make it hard for you to relax and stroke shots.

The great news is that by consciously making adjustments in breathing patterns, you can bring relaxation and optimum focus to your entire competition physical system. Breath can also be used to energize your body between turns and games.

The shot cycle includes several phases in which you can use breathing strategically. In the planning and intention phase, breathing can help you get in touch with the internal part of your own spirit. For instance, in the planning and intention phase, when things are moving too quickly, making yourself stop and breathe can help you organize your thoughts and get you ready to bowl. Breathing can also help during the execution phase. Try inhaling just before the execution and then exhaling as you initiate your pushaway. This can be a great help with timing in this phase. A deep belly breath during the recovery phase is part of what will define physical and emotional clearing.

When we hold our breath, we don't tend to feel our own experiences. By breathing consciously after you roll, you allow yourself to feel your natural emotional response to your shot. Finally, using deep breathing is a way to maximize the clearing and recovery process.

It's just breathing, right? Not really. There is more to using breath to help you bowl. In good tension-reducing breath work, the inhalation goes all the way into the belly. Many people only move their chests when taking a breath, even a deep breath. To learn to belly breathe, put one hand on your chest and one hand on your belly. Try inhaling fully and deeply in such a way that the hand on your belly is moved by air before the hand on your chest. During the exhalation, both hands should move as well. Feel the change in tension levels. Notice the beginning of a warm sense of well-being. This is an easy technique to take to any tournament; it is especially helpful in the clearing and recovery phase. Practice it often to give you a great sense of control over the relaxation response.

Once you have learned the belly breathing technique, move to the next step. Take a deep belly breath, hold it for a mental count of three, and let it go smoothly. Repeat as needed to let go of tension and get a positive internal focus. An effective place to use this, though perhaps with a shorter count, is right before the push away when beginning the approach. Right before pushing off, take a belly breath and initiate the exhalation while taking the first step. Many bowlers make this an important part of the preshot routine. It serves to put the body in flow as well as to shake off distraction. The key to making this work is to go with total commitment to the shot following the exhalation. Linking these two actions will serve as a cueing technique to relax, commit, and go.

Body Relaxation

Relaxing your body can have a profound effect on mental tension. For this reason, the experience of flow and grooving the swing can be influenced by simply learning to relax overly tense muscles. Progressive muscle relaxation (Davis, Robbins Eshelman, and McKay 1995) is a quick, effective way to take tension out of the swing response. This technique, in a radically shorthand version, is especially helpful if you have a difficult time relaxing your grip or allowing a free, loose armswing.

In progressive muscle relaxation (PMR), you briefly overtighten your muscles, then release them into a relaxed state. PMR increases sensitivity to muscular tension and provides a sense of control over tension levels. Although PMR takes a little more time to learn than breathing techniques, once it is learned, it can be used quickly and selectively as needed. By the way, don't practice PMR right after eating because the digestive process can be adversely affected by the alternation of muscle tension and muscle relaxation. Also be especially cautious with neck, back, and other delicate areas to guard against overstraining. You should not feel pain.

Set aside 20 to 30 minutes to learn this skill. Find a relaxing place where you are unlikely to be observed or disturbed. Lie down in a comfortable place or use a reclining chair that has a head support. Once you have learned the technique, you can significantly abbreviate it, use it secretly, and implement it anywhere. Read the PMR sequence that follows, tape it, or have someone else read it while you execute. There are longer versions of PMR (see Davis, Robbins Eshelman, and McKay 1995), but for competition purposes a shorthand version is presented here.

The best way to think of working with the body is to section it into quarters. The first is the hands all the way up the arm. The second is the entire area around the face, head, neck, and shoulders. The third is the trunk, including the stomach and lower back. The fourth is the lower body including the legs, buttocks, and feet. Different bowlers tense different body quadrants, sometimes without even knowing it. Experienced bowlers can easily imagine how each of these areas is involved in the execution of a full-shot delivery.

Tense the targeted muscle or muscle group for 5 to 7 seconds, then relax for 20 to 30 seconds. Don't stay too long in either the tension or relaxation phase. Too much time tensing can create problems, and too much time relaxing will interrupt the flow of the exercise and make it difficult to complete.

Many top bowling coaches emphasize the need to be free and easy with the armswing and have a soft grip with the hands. Sometimes in the heat of competition the grip and arms can unconsciously tighten. Quadrant 1 addresses the arms and hands. Start by adopting an upper-body weightlifter's pose. Tighten both fists, tight, tight, while curling the arms inward to create big biceps. Imagine the biceps muscle like a big softball crawling up the arm. Hold and relax. You can hold for 5 to 7 seconds in practice session, but 1 to 2 seconds should be the maximum during competition.

Many athletes do not recognize how much tension they carry in the jaws, forehead, and other facial areas. Relaxing and relieving these muscles can send a message through the rest of the body and ease the mind as well. Doing PMR for the facial quadrant is like playing five instruments at once. Prune your forehead. Make it as wrinkly as you can. At the same time, gently press your head back and roll it around first one way and then the other. Now make a completely ugly face. Make a wrinkly, pruney face while you frown hard. Your eyes are squinted slits. Your lips are squeezing a tight O. Press your tongue hard to the roof of your mouth, as though you are trying to flatten stiff gum. Hunch your shoulders up to your ears. Tense, relax, and repeat.

Although this exercise may seem odd, practice it. During competition a quick spritz of facial tightening can help your face, body, and emotions calm down. Long competition blocks can be exhausting. If you are holding tension throughout the day, you can really be out of gas at the end. Taking mini relaxation breaks with the body can make all the difference.

Setting a sense of warmth and well-being deep within the trunk of the body is a building block for overall tension regulation. Be careful when addressing the back and lower back. Those with back problems should protect their backs as advised by a physician. Others should take caution not to overstrain. Arch the back as if you were trying to make space for a bowling pin between your back and the chair. Take a full belly breath. Hold, relax, and repeat. Remember to exhale smoothly during the relaxation phase. Again, with practice you can learn to sneak in exercises like this swiftly and privately.

You bowl with your legs. When the legs are wooden or mechanical, timing and leg bend can be jerky and stiff. To do PMR with the lower body, start by straightening the legs from a sitting position. Make duck feet by pressing down with the heels and, without using the hands, pull the toes back toward the face. The shins will feel tight. Hold, relax, and repeat. Next curl the toes under like you are trying to hold a scoring pencil tight with the toes. At the same time, tighten the whole leg from calves to thighs to buttocks. Hold, relax, and repeat. This one is particularly useful during match play when you have two frames to wait for the next turn.

Body relaxation is especially useful when you don't have much time or the pressure is on between shots and games. Remember to tense for a couple of seconds and then absolutely relax the targeted area. Do not overtighten or tighten too long during bowling. The muscles should not get burned out from overtightening. Conversely, the mind and muscles should not get so relaxed in the relaxation phase that you can't get the energy up for competing.

Once sufficiently practiced, this technique can come in handy during the heat of competition. Bowlers can develop the ability to subtly tighten and relax key areas of the body quickly and secretly. The next stage involves personally identifying muscle groups that tend to tighten. With practice, you can even develop an internal image of a stage hypnotist who addresses specific muscle groups with the invitation to "relax, let it all go. You are becoming completely relaxed."

Another way to approach this is to scan the four quadrants in order. Notice if there are any particularly tense areas. Allow the muscle groups to simply relax without doing the tension portion first. Once you have mastered the skill of sensitively detecting and relaxing specific areas, this technique can become among the most useful in competition. It is easily employed, quickly turned on and off, and can be done secretly.

Imagery

Imagery is sometimes confused with visualization. In visualization, you mentally project the future behavior of yourself and the ball. Visualization will be considered in other chapters dealing with shot delivery and spare shooting. It's OK to think of visualization as a form of imagery, so don't get caught up in the terminology.

Imagery can be used in a couple of ways to gain a feeling of mastery during periods of excitement. Imagery, as used here, has to do with creating in your mind a state of comfort in your body and with the competition environment. If anxiety, tension, or overexcitement are pressing before a big competition, or between blocks, imagery is a great way to let out some of the hot tension in the body.

Use your imagination: visual, auditory, and kinesthetic (body feel). Imagine yourself in a safe, wonderful place, wherever works for you. We all have our own personal version of a safe place. For some, it is their beds. For others, it is a warm, secluded beach. It could be sitting in a peaceful mountain glade, or virtually any other place that feels safe, relaxing, and free.

Once you are mentally in your special place, bring all your senses to life—sight, taste, smell, touch, and hearing. What does the air smell like? What is the temperature? If the beach is your special place, imagine the feel of the grains of sand on your fingers and toes, the warmth of the sun, the sounds of birds and waves, and the taste of a cool glass of water or soda on ice. This one is especially useful if you are having difficulty resting or sleeping, which sometimes happens prior to important competitions.

While visualizing, you also can use positive affirmations such as "I am healing," "Warmth and calm are flooding my body and myself," "I am reenergizing," "Health is surging within me," and "I am safe here."

After a few minutes, come back to the present. Notice the feelings of warmth and relaxation. Carry these feelings with you. As with other relaxation and tension-easing techniques, the ability to shift into this mode at will increases dramatically with practice. You can use this skill while waiting for a turn or before the start of an important game. The idea is to induce a warm set of confident feelings on demand.

Effective imagery will relax and energize you even during competition. During competition, even as part of a preshot routine, you can imagine a warm glow within your belly. With this warmth, bring silent self-talk, affirmations around confidence, athleticism, and well-being. When you feel the glow, experience the calmness and centeredness; just exhale and go. It is a wonderful feeling and a big confidence booster to know that you can pull out this powerful tension-combating technique anywhere at any time.

You can target this technique to various parts of your body. To generate power and confidence, imagine relaxation in your arm for a smooth armswing, feelings of power and strength in your legs, softness in your hands for release, and positive emotions in your belly.

Self-Talk

The last relaxation and synchronization technique to learn is silent self-talk or confidence affirmations. When bowlers get into pressure situations in which they have to strike or spare, they often use silent self-talk. This doesn't mean hearing voices or going crazy, just directing the brain to cope positively with the situation.

The worst thing that you can do is to say negative things such as "I have to have this shot," "Don't tense up," "Don't yank the ball," or "Don't squeeze." Often the subconscious mind only registers the action word. The mind doesn't hear "don't yank" (or any other don'ts); instead it focuses on the word *yank* and you end up fighting against the tendency to yank the ball. For this reason self-talk should always be phrased in positive terms.

If you are accustomed to using "nots" or "don'ts," simply pick a phrase that declares the intention of the self-talk in positive terms.

Silent self-talk should lead to the desired focused state. Make yourself aware of your natural self-talk during bowling. This can be easy to notice while practicing or competing. Develop key relaxing phrases such as these:

- I am relaxed and centered.
- I am focused.
- I am a graceful bowler.
- I will hit my target.
- I am centered.

Pick one or two that will most assist the flow of your bowling. Keep the phrases handy. Practice with them. Let focus and feelings shift with the use of positive self-affirming talk. This technique is silent, effective, and always available in a pinch.

One vital note: Affirmative self-talk must not turn into a con or sales job. It only works if you are willing to wholeheartedly go into the state of being that is suggested by your words. You must first believe it. Here is the order for self-talk: Believe it. Say it. Be it. Do it!

DEALING WITH ADVERSE CONDITIONS

Every bowler has had the frustrating experience of struggling to shake off the distractions and disturbances of different competition situations, whether it is noise, messed-up oil patterns, rude or aggressive players, or the pressures of high-stakes competition. All bowlers want to learn to deal effectively with anything thrown at them.

Bowlers practice to be able to repeat the best of training efforts in the heat of competition. Many bowlers are distracted when they get to the bowling center on game day and discover that conditions, internal and external, have shifted away from their comfort zones.

During one of the professional tour stops in 2001, I heard horror stories from competitors about having to deal with ultra-sticky approaches. The athletes had to make severe adjustments in the normal slide part of their delivery. It was bad enough that the physical demands of the lane approaches required a different kind of game. Just as significant was the earthquake that several professionals felt in their competition psyches.

League and tournament surprises lie like trolls under a bridge waiting to pounce. Bowlers will benefit greatly by understanding the sources of their discomfort and distraction, as well as by having effective strategies at their fingertips for handling disruptions.

Psychological Muscle

To feel confident, effective, and masterful, you must understand two psychological elements. First, confidence and feelings of security come with being able to have a sense of prediction and control over what will happen in the bowling environment and during the shot cycle. A sense of control and predictability lends strong feelings of stability to any athlete (see chapter 3).

The second element is concentration and focus. Many bowlers wait for the bowling environment to fall into line with their personal needs, wants, and comfort zones. True psychological muscle comes with being able to focus and concentrate in any condition or circumstance.

Consider again. Imagine the lives of our cave ancestors. They had to be able to read all kinds of signs that would tell them a dangerous animal was near, an enemy was prowling, or nasty weather was approaching. By learning to read the signs correctly, they were able to receive advance warning of danger. Advance warning was only one part of the equation, however. They also had to have strategies for dealing with whatever dangers occurred. These strategies kept them from having to live in anxiety and fear all the time. They knew that they had options in the face of difficulty. They could not control what happened, but they could control how they responded to it.

Think of the opposite situation. Someone who had no way to sense that something was wrong, dangerous, or out of whack would have to be tense and vigilant all the time to watch out for whatever might happen next. Worse yet, not having any coping options for handling tigers, attacking armies, or super-sticky approaches could lead to all kinds of mental and emotional upheaval. When we have no effective action to take, feelings of tension and fear emerge. The result can be unpredictable errant shots, aggravation, and concerns about future competition conditions.

When you are unable to predict or control what is going to happen, you end up with anxiety and panic. If this state of affairs continues, you will eventually become discouraged and may give up. There are several ways to prevent or escape this undesirable condition. Chapters 3 and 4 give you important points of focus for creating a preshot routine and attending to each part of the shot cycle. Once you have absolute faith in yourself for executing your shot cycle from an internal reference point, the impact of external irritants and distractions will diminish significantly.

Escape the Shoulds

Before we discuss a vital concept in adjusting to adverse playing circumstances, let's take a fresh look at what *adverse* actually means. The *American Heritage Dictionary* defines *adverse* as "antagonistic in design or effect," "contrary to one's interests or welfare," or "in an opposite or opposing direction or position." The word *adversity* is defined as "a state of hardship or affliction," "misfortune," or "a calamitous event."

These definitions offer insight into what it means to players when they encounter adverse conditions. An adverse condition can be a challenging or new sport, an oil pattern, sticky or slick approaches, dirty back-ends that slide the pins instead of trip them, an opponent who slaps his hands in your face after a strike, or any other environmental condition. Adversity on the lanes feels that way because it is experienced as calamitous, hardship and affliction, or antagonistic. Simply put, something is going on that you don't like.

The overwhelming thought process for bowlers who struggle with unpleasant conditions and hardships is that the difficulties somehow should not be there. The belief that life is supposed to be other than it actually is gets bowlers frazzled, frustrated, angry, and upset. Here are some of the classic beliefs of bowlers:

- There *should* be obvious breakpoints on freshly oiled lanes.
- The shot *should* be easier, or harder, or not so easy for lefties, or not so easy for righties.
- Other bowlers *should* wait their turns and not jump up on the approaches when you should be next.
- The bowling center *should* be warmer, colder, quieter, better ventilated, better equipped, and have slower racks.

Notice the many occurrences of the word *should* in the preceding list. Instead of dealing with the *is*-ness of the situation, the bowler is dealing with one or more shoulds. The shoulds will kill concentration, feelings of well-being, and focused wholehearted deliveries while bowling. Of course, the upside for many bowlers is that adverse conditions give them a good story about why they did not win or score well.

The first step in dealing with adverse conditions is to quickly assess whether you can change or control anything in the bowling environment that is thwarting you. Then decide if it is worth acting on. If you decide that you cannot control the conditions, the next step is to come into absolute acceptance of the situation. You need to ask yourself only one question: What do I need to do to perform my best under these circumstances? If you are busy constructing reasons for not excelling, you have already lost the game, regardless of the final score. Accepting what cannot be changed and then deciding how to cope best is generally the most effective course of action. When you learn to do this, you will come to understand that many of the adverse conditions you encounter are really problems in your own thinking instead of problems in the world.

Escape the *shoulds* by accepting what you can't change about the alley environment, such as other bowlers on the lanes.

To summarize, step 1 is to identify the source of frustration or irritation. Notice where the should or shouldn't is in your thinking. Step 2 is to drop the should. Life is the way it is. Decide whether you can take any effective course of action to correct the situation. Step 3 is to take action, if you decide you can effect a change in the circumstances. Step 4 is to make a decision to accept the circumstances and go forth with adaptive adjustments. Step 5 is to assess whether you are effective in your coping decisions and perhaps try another adjustment. Check your thinking. Are you still living in shoulds? If so, knock it off.

It is OK to have preferences about how life ought to be, just not demands. The rest of the world tends to be spectacularly oblivious to most of our requirements for order and care-taking. Alcoholics Anonymous has a saying they call the Serenity Prayer. It requires only minor adjustment to turn it into a bowler's prayer:

> Please give me the strength to change the things I can, the courage to handle the things I cannot change, and the wisdom to know the difference.

Work Outside Your Comfort Zone

The next important mental set is to get used to playing outside your comfort zone of normal thoughts and feelings.

People loosely throw around the term *comfort zone* as if there is a common understanding about what this entails. To visualize your comfort zone, imagine two parallel lines (see figure 5.1). On the inside are all the things that allow for comfort. The list includes familiarity, normalcy, predictability, the usual state of affairs, and generally "the known." On the outside of the lines is unpredictability, fresh and new experiences, risk, feelings, life, and growth. The problem with playing outside of the lines is that it can be unsettling if you are not used to playing there. The problem with playing inside the lines is that unless normal conditions are always present, you can get jerked out of common and usual expectations and end up feeling helpless, overwhelmed, and ineffective.

To improve, grow, and prepare to master all competition situations, you must embrace play outside of the comfort zone. The same rules apply in all of life. There is no coincidence there.

A customer quote is posted in one of the pro shops at the National Bowling Stadium in Reno that reads: "I like to stand with my left foot on the center dot in the middle and throw over the second arrow." Even though the lanes were oiled for a different shot, the bowler was demanding a ball that would let him stay in his comfort zone. This real-life quote serves to remind the pro shop instructors of how wedded to playing a specific part of the lane many bowlers tend to be.

As any moderately experienced bowler knows, lane oil patterns and bowling conditions can vary greatly from tournament to tournament, from lane to lane, and even from frame to frame. If you get attached to playing a certain line with a certain ball

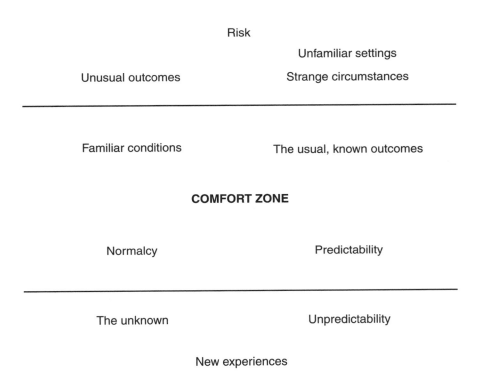

Risk

Unfamiliar settings

Unusual outcomes   Strange circumstances

Familiar conditions   The usual, known outcomes

COMFORT ZONE

Normalcy   Predictability

The unknown   Unpredictability

New experiences

Figure 5.1 Inside the comfort zone are all the things that are familiar and easy. Outside the comfort zone lie risks and unpredictable situations.

every time, you will suffer badly with erratic ball reactions, poor scores, and increasing self-doubt. The only way to succeed is to be willing to play with different equipment, on different parts of the lane, and using different hand positions and ball speeds.

For most people, dealing with adverse conditions means being pushed out of the comfortable and familiar. Examine when you bowl your best. For some people, it is practice time alone. For others, it is league play. Some people need to have a coach present. Beware of what happens when other variables present themselves.

Bowlers err when they try to force conditions back into the comfort zone, where everything is normal and easy. They need quiet conditions, become irritable when lane courtesies are not observed, and insist on changing balls and speeds to keep from moving their strike line.

We develop the flexibility to move out of our comfort zones in much the same way that we develop physical flexibility. When young gymnasts are learning to do the splits, they have to stretch several times a day, pushing their legs just a little bit past the previous limit. Bowlers must develop similar drills. For example, try playing strike shots over every single arrow in practice. Make yourself hit the pocket rolling over each arrow as a wind-up or wind-down exercise. In practice, recreate troublesome situations. Bowl next to recreational bowlers who don't know bowling etiquette. Play entire games with a plastic ball that has very little reaction.

Another technique you may try is a preventative measure called *stress inoculation*. Just like having a flu shot before flu season, it is possible to prepare the psychological immune system before a tournament. Before a given league or tournament play imagine any of the possible distractions or irritants that will face you. Most bowlers can identify their weak links in terms of competition stresses. Have a plan ready for how to respond to each of them, as well as a plan to stay focused on your shot cycle no matter what. That way you won't be emotionally off guard when things happen outside your comfort zone.

The Art of Concentrating Anywhere

Concentrate harder! Concentrate better! These are the directions flustered bowlers give themselves to regain a sense of control in the game. Beefing up concentration is a great idea for reestablishing control, but most people do not really know how to do it.

If a coach asked you to concentrate harder during the 10th frame of an important match, what would you do? You would have to do more than just treat the shot as important. The first step is to have a clear understanding of the meaning of concentration in competition. Without getting this part straight, it will be nearly impossible to grab this tiger by the tail. You might actually lose concentration in your attempt to figure out what to do to concentrate more effectively!

Concentration is the ability to hold attention on specific aspects of thoughts, feelings, and the physical game. To concentrate, you have to minimize the distraction of irrelevant and useless thoughts, sights, sounds, and other sensations. Imagine catching a single snowflake on your tongue out of an entire blowing snowstorm. Concentration is holding focus on that one flake no matter how many other snowflakes are flying past.

Look at an example closer to problems in bowling. Think of air traffic controllers who have to direct planes to land. No matter who might be talking in the background, no matter what their dinner plans are for the evening, no matter who might be observing the quality of their work, they have to accomplish the job of safely guiding an airplane. At the same time, they are aware of weather, other airplanes, and ground conditions.

Concentration in bowling is like guiding the ball onto the lanes and safely to the breakpoint and ultimately into the pocket (or over the mark on a spare shot). The bowler is the executive decision maker concerning thoughts, the mark, delivery timing, hand position, or any other key point of attention.

Let's see how well you do on a concentration and focus training exercise. You may discover some things about where you stand with elements of these skills.

1. Set aside an area, preferably a relatively quiet room, where you can participate fully in this exercise.

2. Set a time limit of five minutes.

3. Get relaxed and comfortable.

4. Develop a point of focus. This can be on something external like a bowling ball, a picture, or any chosen object. The focus point can also be internal as in meditation—a special word, mental picture, or thought.

5. Be aware of any thoughts that come into your mind. Include other sights and sounds as well. Notice anything from music, to clocks ticking, to the colors in the room, to thoughts of bowling. It doesn't matter.

6. Gently bring your attention back to the central focus thought or object. Hold your attention only on the focus thought or object. If another sensation or thought presents itself, simply recognize it, name it for what it is, and then bring your attention back to the focus thought. Be aware that the most common intruding thoughts will include boredom, silliness, questioning the value of the exercise, and thinking about other things. This is normal. These

distracting thoughts are just like the ones that occur in competition.

7. Return to a full general awareness of the whole room.

This focus training exercise is incredibly easy to pack up and take with you. Practice it frequently to enhance your ability to concentrate and control internal conditions anywhere. To illustrate, consider these parallels to the challenges in competition bowling:

1. The quiet room is like the bowling center.
2. Getting into the concentration exercise equals getting ready to bowl on the lanes.
3. Relaxing and developing a point of focus equals breathing and starting the preshot routine.
4. Holding the point of focus equals having the intention to focus on the game or your mark.
5. Allowing yourself to become aware of other sights and sounds and then bringing your attention back to the point of focus is exactly what you need to do on the approach and delivery; for example, you might notice the background talking, noises, and internal thoughts that intrude.
6. Shifting your attention back to delivering the shot is like refocusing in the sitting exercise.
7. Returning your awareness to the room is equivalent to the wind-down after the delivery when you return to the settee area or let down for a moment before preparing for the next shot.

The point is not to forcefully screen out distractions. Such an effort will only add to your tension and stress. Bowling can be instead like driving a car. You can focus on the road without erasing the landscape. You are the ultimate selector of thoughts, ideas, and sensations.

Adverse conditions are going to happen, so it is best to be ready with a plan. Consider ahead of time the distractions or situations that may unsettle you, and plan a strategy for dealing with them. The goal is to normalize your reactions so that you do not waste time and energy cursing circumstances during competition.

You can't screen out distractions, but you can plan how you will cope with them.

Remember, concentration is simply the ability to bring the energy of your attention to something and hold it just long enough to accomplish the task. Don't make the mistake of thinking this means being absolutely oblivious to everything else. On the contrary, even when concentration is at an all-time high, the mind can still register other sights, sounds, and thoughts.

Some bowlers mistakenly believe that concentration means trying harder (Kubistant 1986). In fact, trying harder only makes many bowlers tense, without knowing exactly what to do more, or harder, or better. The result frequently is the conversion of personal intensity into tension. The muscles tighten, the flow of the approach and armswing is compromised, and the results are poor pin fall and crazy spare configurations.

Concentration really involves channeling mental and physical resources to the needs of the moment, whether those needs are listening to a coach or delivering a strike shot. Yes, bring intensity. However, intensity means total intention (commitment to execute) plus enough energy to get the job done. When you add concentration to intention and energy, you achieve focus.

Think of what the word *focus* means in photography. Imagine a photographer covering a bowling event. First the photographer observes a lane. He or she then aims the camera down the lane from the bowler's point of view, adjusting the lens so that only the ball, the mark, and the pins are in focus. It doesn't matter what else might exist outside of the physical and mental target. Anything else that was once in the field of vision becomes irrelevant. When the photographer is ready, he or she tightens the focus on one spot and takes the photo. Restated in bowling terms, when you are ready, you zero your awareness in on a key thought, visual mark, or physical sensation and complete the delivery sequence. If you have visualized the shot fully before execution, all the better.

Here are the steps for concentrating effectively:

1. Point your attention to the general object or area of interest (the lanes, pins, key thoughts, etc.).

2. Narrow your attention to the finer internal and external details such as your preshot routine, your breathing, or the lane markers.

3. Make adjustments in your stance, timing, hand position, and so on.

4. Accept background sounds, smells, and movements, and then let them fade.

5. Proceed with your action sequence with complete commitment to wholehearted execution.

Let's look at the steps using a problem that occurs frequently on the professional tour. The bowler arrives at the tournament with a good idea of how to play the lanes after a run-through practice session the previous day in which the oil pattern was supposedly laid out the same as it would be in the tournament. However, today the warm-up period is a struggle. The early balls don't finish in the pocket. The bowler leaves a 2-8-10 split, then a 1-2-4 pin washout.

This is the choice point. The bowler can succumb to all kinds of careless thoughts, feelings, and reactions. There can be anger and thoughts that the tournament coordinators changed the lanes unfairly, or there can be renewed determination to make the original plan work, including ball selection and lane play strategy. All bowlers have experienced these thoughts at one time or another.

The bowler's other choice is to go through with the following coping process:

1. Drop all of the shoulds about how things are, or were, supposed to be.

2. Take a fresh assessment of what seems to be called for given the current condition and make a decision about how best to play the lanes. *See* the lanes. Make ball choices and breakpoint best guesses.

3. Make the necessary adjustments in stance, hand position, armswing, and so on. Decide to go forth wholeheartedly. Continue with the preshot routine. (Notice that all of this activity takes place in stage 1 of the shot cycle.)

4. Let the background sights, smells, and movements fade into the background. Stay with the thinking, seeing, and physical sensation that are the foreground of the picture—for example, visualize body position, ball path, and rotation.

5. Commit to the plan completely (stage 2 of the shot cycle).

When moving from general observations (lanes, pins, the movement of other bowlers) to the plan for making the strike or spare, including shifting to internal focus (balance, cue thought, preshot activities, release), allow fears, concerns, and distractions to diminish naturally. They will, if you let them.

The Mental Game Myth

One of the most confusing and destructive mental game myths is that we should make bad thoughts or feelings go away. Many athletes have interpreted training on self-talk and positive thinking to mean that they are not supposed to allow certain thoughts and sensations to be present. This is almost impossible to do.

Consider this real-life example. An accomplished bowler prepares to concentrate, go through the preshot routine, and deliver a good shot, but the bowling center is full of potentially distracting sights and sounds. Other bowlers are up on the approaches. People are talking. Pins are cracking. The bowler can wait for the world to pay some respect by settling down and being quiet, but this does not even happen on the professional bowlers' TV show. The bowler can attempt to try to fight off intruding thoughts, perhaps saying internally, "Don't notice those other bowlers. Go away, self-doubt thoughts. Go away, concerns about release."

Here is the problem. Anything athletes try not to do, or think about, tends to dominate their thoughts. For example, if you tell yourself, "Don't see the bowler on the next approach," your brain naturally continues to register the person on the next approach, the one thing you told yourself not to do! This is true for thoughts, feelings, and anything happening in the bowling center. If you were told never again to notice anyone two lanes away in either direction no matter what, a problem would immediately present itself. You might be able to keep your vision absolutely forward, but you would actually be more aware of other bowlers. In effect, trying not to see the other bowlers would control you!

Disturbing and distracting thoughts are like a dragon flying around the brain. If you try to fight the dragon, it sticks around, pokes back, and spits flames at you. If you simply say, "I see you, dragon. Go ahead and fly around. I have other places to put my attention," then the dragon fades into the background. The dragon is still there, but it isn't relevant to your immediate thoughts.

The best coping strategy is to decide what to think about or focus on. Then, when a disturbing thought or awareness presents itself, simply put your energy into returning to the original point of focus. Do not try to make the thought go away. Just like the dragon, the negative thought only strengthens when you concentrate on it.

You do not have to worry about intruding thoughts as long as you trust your ability to return repeatedly to the chosen area of focus. This is how step 2 of the coping process, including the preshot routine, serves you. Background thoughts, external activities, and other adverse conditions can be like the crackles and pops heard on an old phonograph album or cassette tape. You can let the pops and snaps distract you, or you can turn your full attention to the music, acknowledging but ignoring the extraneous sounds.

Another example can be found in the study of meditation. Students of meditation sometimes have problems with intruding thoughts. When sitting in silence, all kinds of thoughts and feelings can creep in. The instruction for the meditation practitioner is not to try to make the thoughts and distractions go away. Rather, students are taught to return their attention to the mantra word or sensory focus to which they are attending. Whatever is resisted persists in consciousness!

Learning to concentrate is easy and can be practiced whenever you practice bowling. When setting up for a shot, pick an area of focus (free armswing, balance at the line, uninterrupted preshot routine, etc.). Next, become aware of other sights, sounds, and smells. Perhaps engage in conversation for a moment. Then return to your chosen thoughts and commitment to action. With consistent practice, your ability to do this well will skyrocket.

An advantage of allowing other thoughts, sights, and sounds to register in consciousness is that it will allow you to make adjustments as needed to deal with circumstances. This adapted focus is a highly trainable skill and should be one of the most trusted weapons in the mental game arsenal.

A training game called combat bowling is a great way to practice staying focused. Find a bowling buddy or a coach who will help you. The task of your partner is to do everything possible, short of physical threat or contact, to distract, disturb, and disorient you. Sometimes this can be funny, sometimes deadly serious. Let the person know your weak link. If it is someone jumping up on the next pair, have your partner do that. If it is making noise, have your partner yell out your name. If it is other competitors' behavior, have your partner trash talk, challenge, or whatever it is that gets your goat. Practicing this way periodically is another form of inoculation that will protect you when the real deal presents itself.

You now have an arsenal of training techniques for dealing with any kind of adverse conditions. Practice and rehearsal is critical. Once you gain mastery over the shoulds, the distractions, and other unpredictable and troublesome events, your confidence about handling competition life will surge!

chapter
6

THE SECRET TO MAKING SPARES

The success or failure of any tournament or league night experience often boils down to spare shooting. Strikes come and go, but perfect games are still statistically unusual events. Everyone who picks up a ball at the beginning of competition can expect to have to make some critical spares during the match.

Champions in any sport have simple formulas for executing key skills at critical times. In fact, you can probably think of several formulas for success that you use in your everyday life. When you have a formula for success—in any activity—you have no need to rely on special gifts or talents. Whether it is making chocolate chip cookies or toning abdominal muscles, if you follow a good formula, the end product is just about ensured.

The good news is that there is a formula for spare shooting that produces great results. Be warned: A shift in normal thinking may be required. You will need a true openness to adopting a new perspective on how to succeed. Although this formula may look elementary, it is critical for mastering the mental game. Learn this elegant secret inside and out, and it will never desert you in a time of need.

Notice that I use the term *formula* and not *system* at this point. For the bowler looking for a reliable spare-shooting plan, I will present an earthquake-proof spare system later in this chapter.

Many strategies exist for moving right or left off the strike line or lining up with a plastic ball on preestablished marks. Most physical spare-shooting directions are simple and effective. The problem that competitors encounter is not that they don't know what ball to throw, or where to throw it. The problem is that they often overthink and tense up when shooting single pins and combination spares that are well within their ability level.

Spare-Shooting Formula

Bowlers use many strategies for handling spare-shooting anxiety. Deep breathing, muscle relaxation, visualization, and self-talk all have proven success. In this chapter, some of these techniques will be added to the mix for effective spare shooting. However, beyond all of the classic techniques is the following ultimate formula:

Staying in the present + intention + mechanism = ultimate spare shooting

At first glance, this simple formula probably does not seem earth-shattering. It may even seem obvious. Once translated into bowling terms, however, it will be the only spare-shooting magic you will need. Welcome to one of the keys to the competition universe.

To unlock this formula, you must fully understand and internalize the terms.

Stay in the Present

When your strike shot does not net 10 in the pit, you will likely experience a flash of disappointment. The thoughts and self-statements that come to mind at this point will significantly affect the next ball you roll, either positively or negatively. Here are some examples of negative thoughts:

- Upset thoughts and feelings related to throwing the bad shot
- Concern that a strike was very important in that particular frame for personal or team scores
- Pressured thoughts about having missed the same or different spares
- Anxiety about the importance of making the spare
- Lack of confidence in executing the spare shot

Instead of wallowing in negative thoughts, you can choose instead to use positive thoughts and self-statements, which will lead to confidence in your spare strategy, trust in your execution, mental preparation for throwing a good shot, and mental adjustments to physical setup and lane play based on the strike shot. Positive self-statements will be described in greater detail later in this chapter.

At the deepest level, there is a fundamental distinction between great spare shooters and the rest of the field. Those who deliver are able to stay in the present when they go to execute. You have three options: living in the past, present, or future frames. Anytime you do not play the game in the present frame, your spare shooting is at great risk.

Think of the frames of the game as frames in a movie. Each of those frames is broken further into split frames for the first and, if needed, second shots. Past frame orientation can be identified by some key symptoms. Watch out for thoughts of unfair pin fall, anger, irritability, hopelessness, or helplessness to carry the pins. Frustration is a mental and emotional clue that you are not shaking off disappointing bowling results. Beware of the *shoulds* discussed in chapter 5. Do not get caught up in the outrage of having left an unfair pin or combination spare. Also be careful about living overlong in self-punishment or anger at having thrown an errant shot or having read the lane conditions incorrectly. Any of these thinking patterns will trap you in past frame orientation.

Future frame problems show up as anxiety, fear, distrust, or a lack of confidence about your ability to deliver a good shot. Even excitement about the upcoming shot can be a way of living in the future if it is not managed. In a nutshell, any attention to the consequences of leaving, or having to pick up, a spare is living in past or future frames.

Flow, peak performance, and maximum effectiveness come with living in the present frame. In this frame, you can briefly acknowledge any thoughts or feelings about leaving a spare and having to pick it up. Beyond that, the shot cycle, including the preshot routine and awareness of the ball, the body, and the lanes, has to be in the present tense.

Imagine being the captain of a ship leaving shore. Thinking about leaving pins standing and getting bothered about it is like sailing out to sea while still staring at the shore. This is an incredibly ineffective way to steer a ship. Thinking about the consequences of what will happen if you make or miss the spare is like focusing on what lies in store for you over the horizon. This still puts the ship in danger of hitting rocks and obstacles in the present harbor. The best way to steer a ship through a harbor is to stand in the wheelhouse and be aware of the conditions and realities of the moment. Staying completely aware of what is happening now affords the best chance of successful navigation.

If you are bemoaning the fact that you threw an errant shot or feel cheated about not carrying the rack, you are living in the past, crippling yourself, sailing the ship by looking backward. If you focus on the importance of the spare, either for success or scores, or to avoid embarrassment, you risk increasing your anxiety and losing your composure. This is like staring at the horizon. Both scenarios can result in your losing the feel for the shot and missing the spare.

For effective spare shooting, you need to keep your mind on the present shot. Let go of the errant ball that left the split and focus on what you have to do now to make the spare.

The only place to be is right here, right now. Don't bother chasing away past and future thoughts. Those thoughts are like little cartoon bubbles floating past the inner mind. Simply decide to orient to what is happening now. A great way to do this is to decide to focus on two aspects of the spare shot: the shot cycle, including the preshot routine, and the finish.

Each bowler needs to have a regular and reliable sequence of thoughts and behaviors that precedes every practice and game shot. Staying with this preshot sequence can be incredibly calming and reassuring.

The second key to staying present and aware in spare shooting is to give extra attention to finishing the shot well. Make a decision to deliver the shot with great follow-through, balance, and intention, which we will discuss in the next section. If you are fully committed and aware and feel good about what you brought to finish the shot, then you are probably living spare shooting in the present frame.

Have Intention

Most people use the word *intention* all the time without really being clear about its true meaning. Many athletes make the mistake of confusing ideas such as hoping, wanting, and wishing with the power of intention. Athletes who count on ideas like hoping, wanting, and wishing are likely to go broke when it comes to competition rewards. Intention as defined here is the absolute commitment to getting something done, regardless of the circumstances.

Most people make commitments that evaporate when significant hurdles get in the way. Just look at New Year's resolutions. The best-sellers are losing weight, exercising, and quitting smoking. Unfortunately, an extremely low percentage of people who make New Year's resolutions keep their word. All kinds of things come up, such as feelings of hunger, fatigue, time constraints, force of habit, and so forth. The bottom line is that something else becomes more powerful and compelling than the original promise.

To make the spare-shooting formula work, you must understand total intention and commitment. Real intention is the deepest of deep-seated desires. It is the one thing that will keep you going no matter what feelings or obstacles appear. You either have committed intention or you don't.

In terms of self-talk, the mind really hears whatever comes after the word *I*. For instance, if you say to yourself, "I hope I make this four pin," your mind focuses on hoping instead of on confidence. The same thing applies to "I want," "I fear," and "I wish." Now notice the difference between those statements and these simple statements: "I will execute this shot," or "I intend to roll a great shot." The mind can now focus on "I will" or "I intend." An authentic self-declaration of intention has the best chance of getting the subconscious mind to respond.

Without true intention, the mental game can get rocked by overthinking, fear, and anxiety, as well as by external factors such as noise and other distractions. Without this essential ingredient, the normal earthquakes of training and competition will shake the spare shooting right out of you.

You can identify whether you have true intention to get better at spares. Simply look at your results. See what you are doing to excel at this skill. Intention and results go together like the head and tail of a coin. Look at other places in life to see the truth in this. Losing weight or quitting smoking are good examples. At the most basic level, if a person did not complete the promise to cut pounds or quit cigarettes, that person did not have true intention. The individual may have had all the right mechanisms, such as membership in a weight-loss clinic and nicotine patches, but the only thing that counts is the result. No habit change shows a lack of intention.

Many would argue, "Wait, this person really did want to quit smoking or lose weight." Remember that wanting, wishing, and trying do not represent true intention. At best, it can be said that wanting and wishing are intention-lite. They work until significant resistance appears. In the formula, intention is far deeper even than willpower. For those who do not reach their goals, perhaps a more compelling intention secretly appeared: being comfortable, satisfying cravings, or responding to a habit. Real intention always makes itself known.

At the level of shot execution, intention is both subtle and clear. State your intention to focus, visualize the shot picture, and freely allow your arm to swing with total follow-through. Then it is a simple thing to observe from both the inside and the outside whether or not you brought your intention to life. This is a black-or-white issue, all or none, one or 10. You surrender to your intention to be free with the shot, or you go with an intention to protect yourself and play it safe. Ironically, it is far safer to go for greatness in execution than it is to tighten up and try to aim.

Getting away from single frames, there are thousands of bowling examples. Here is a training example. Take a 200-average bowler on a standard house block oil condition. If the bowler states a true intention of raising the league average by five or more pins, we can only know the commitment to this intention by the result. A person with true intention will do whatever is needed to achieve the goal. Money is no object to a committed person. Time is no barrier. Nothing will stand in the way of success, even if it means hiring a personal coach or sport psychologist. Such a person does whatever is needed to achieve the result. That is the meaning of true intention. Everything else is a weak substitute.

Use the Right Mechanism

People often think *mechanism* means a machine or a machine part. In a way, a mechanism is a tool, the means to the end of any effort. It is the way that you get where you are going. In bowling, mechanisms include, among other things, balls and ball surfaces, drillings, and weights; hand positions; ball speed and rotation; spare lines; shoes; wrist braces; tacky and slippery substances for hands and shoes; towels; and mental game tools such as visualization, preshot routines, shot cycles, and relaxation.

A mechanism is any of the hundreds of methods and tools that will take you to magnificent spare shooting. There is never just one mechanism for any spare, or any bowling goal, for that matter.

Bowlers frequently confuse mechanism with what it takes to score and make spares. They think that if they just have the right ball, the right spare strategy, and the right preshot routine, they will succeed. Advertising works the same way. Advertising tells us that if we drive the right car, drink the right beer, or use the right credit card, life will turn out grandly. Ads say nothing about making things happen on your own. In bowling terms, the right ball won't shoot your spares; you have to shoot them.

Champions are people who can overcome feelings, fear, and external conditions to get results. Pick a mechanism—equipment or physical technique—and bring full intention to making it work for you. If it doesn't work, reevaluate the mechanism, make a change as needed, and go at it with full intention again. The correct application of intention plus mechanism will overcome bowling balls, lane conditions, and even pesky bowling gods.

Make Spare Shooting Work

Intention plus mechanism plugs in perfectly to spare shooting. To accomplish great spare shooting, you must first get some basic mechanisms in place. Decide whether or not to get a spare ball. Establish a basic spare system, such as the one developed by coach Susie Minshew, shown on page 96. Determine which spare to throw straight and which to hook.

Let's look at how total and complete intention opens up spare shooting. Many bowlers mistakenly think that the more they need to make a shot, the better they will do. It is true that for some competitors, focus increases with importance. If we look closely, however, we see that what is really enhanced is commitment to focus, not shot-throwing ability.

Success in spare shooting, as in every other part of the game, depends on committing to the right things. Often competitors commit to calming down and trying to make nervous or anxious feelings go away. Another frequent effort is to banish distracting or negative thoughts. This directs mental and emotional energy to trying to make a thought or feeling vanish. Not only is this extremely difficult to do, but it is also a detour from positive and useful intentional thoughts.

The best plan is to pick the most powerful intentions to match your spare-shooting plan. You can bring full intention and commitment to your approach to the spare and the foul line. With all your thoughts and impulses, no matter what you might be feeling, commit to one or more of the following principles.

Commit to swinging freely at all costs. When the stakes are high or when the spare is particularly challenging, the tendency is to try to point or fit the shot. Being careful only serves to change your natural stroke and to threaten results instead of

Swing freely when shooting the spare. Being careful alters your natural stroke, increasing the risk of leaving a pin.

ensuring them. A free armswing gets the ball on line with the maximum amount of energy and the greatest chance of going where you want to send it. If making a spare or having to strike to win is the situation, bowlers become increasingly vulnerable to trying to control the entire ball path. Muscling and pulling the ball down puts you at greater risk for errant shots.

Remember, you can control only where you send the ball on the lane. With a reactive ball you can send it to the breakpoint with a certain speed, roll, and tilt. After the ball makes the turn at the breakpoint, it's all physics.

Decide on the spare line and trust it. Once you have decided where to throw the ball, all debate is over. Unconscious questions about whether it is the best line will cause subtle deviations and corrections as you approach the foul line. Every time you leave a spare in practice, you can be thankful for the opportunity to practice this one as if you were in the most intense competition. The principle remains the same in any situation.

Commit to rolling with heart and spirit. Spare shooting can be analyzed from top to bottom. Not coincidentally, that is frequently the problem—thinking instead of accessing the feel that the trained mind and body can deliver. The issue of heart and spirit can be determined by a single question: Did I like who I was when I threw that shot? Or in simpler terms, go for it in such a way that you feel OK after the ball leaves your hand, even before you know the result. After you roll the shot, you should feel that you could spin around, face the settee area, and say, "That's the man/woman I am," and feel good about it. If you are an overthinking, tight, careful person while you bowl, you will not want to sign your name to the shot, whether you make or miss it.

Finish well. If there is only one aspect of the physical game that intersects perfectly with the mental game of spare shooting, it is finishing the shot. The commitment to completing the shot with a free armswing, easy release, and finishing pose can clear out the tendency for overthinking and plow through anxiety, allowing for proper mechanics without even having to think about it.

This is an aspect of spare shooting that you can easily observe and reinforce during practice. It takes discipline to keep the finish of the swing in the forefront of your thoughts. Something about the commitment to finish well keeps you from shoveling, pulling, or otherwise muscling the shot. In addition, if you have difficulty balancing and finishing well, you have information that something is amiss earlier in the shot sequence.

Make the choice. You have to decide up front that you will demonstrate guts, athleticism, and commitment to the motion of the free armswing. Make this commitment no matter what thoughts or feelings might be swirling around in your head. There is always a fundamental choice: Do you try to make pressured, analytic, or questioning thoughts and feelings go away, or do you throw all of your mental energy into how to feel about the act of shooting the spare before you even roll the shot? You can do a sort of spare-shooting inoculation by making this decision before ever stepping up on the approach. Choose guts, grace, and athleticism over carefulness. This commitment will actually raise your spare-shooting percentage.

Spare Systems by Susie Minshew, USA Gold Coach

There are many spare systems to choose from. The most important thing is to pick one you feel comfortable and confident using.

There are 1,023 different kinds of spares. Figuring out where to stand for every conceivable lane condition and pin combination would be truly overwhelming. In order to keep things simple, the number can be reduced to four spare lines: the 4/7, the 2-pin or any of its combinations, the 3-pin or any of its combinations, and the 6/10.

In this discussion, we work from the point of view of a right-handed bowler. Left-handers should simply reverse the information. Each of the following systems assumes that you walk parallel to your intended ball path. If you are throwing left to right, you walk left to right, and vice versa.

System One

This system assumes the use of a ball or ball roll that will allow for a relatively straight path to and through the target. This allows for minimal adjustments based on lane conditions.

Former Team USA member and PBA champion Chris Barnes uses a plastic ball for most of his spare shooting, even on combination spares. Similarly, many professionals feel that using a ball that takes lane conditions out of consideration is the smartest move.

A method commonly used by elite bowlers is to shoot all spares over the fourth arrow, the one in the middle. For every spare, you move your feet until you cross the fourth arrow going toward the intended target. For both 6- and 10-pin spares on the right, stand with the inside of your slide foot on board 35. You may need to adjust by a board or two depending on your body size and shape. Visualize the shot going across board 20 (the middle arrow) toward the 6 and 10 pins.

For the 3-pin spare on the right side, simply move your feet right to board 33. Draw a line in your mind's eye through the middle arrow to the center of the 3-pin. Of course you have to make sure that you walk directly in a straight line toward your target on each of these spare shots. For left side spares, reverse the system.

When shooting 4- or 7-pin spares, start with the slide foot on board 19. Visualize the line through board 20 to the space between the 4 and 7. For the 2-pin spare start on board 22.

System Two

System two follows the same principles as system one; however, this system moves you outside to cross the lane with more angle.

For a right-handed bowler shooting either a 4- or 7-pin spare, start with the slide foot on board 10. The target is the second arrow. Your slide foot will end up around board 14.

For the 2-pin or any of its combinations, start your foot on board 15. The target remains the second arrow.

For the 3-pin or any of its combinations, start your slide foot on board 30. The target is the third arrow. Slide on 29.

For the 6-pin, 10-pin, or 6/10 spare, start your slide foot on 35. The target is right between the third and fourth arrows, right over board 17. On this spare, you can take the third and fourth arrows and mentally tilt them toward the 6/10. This helps create a picture of a trough leading directly to the 6/10.

For left-handers the system is mirrored to the other side of the lane. For 4-pin, 7-pin, or 4/7 spares, start with the slide foot on 35. The target is the trough between the third and fourth arrows. Slide on 32. For the 2-pin or any of its combinations, start the slide foot on board 30. The target is the third arrow. Slide on 29. For the 3-pin or any of its combinations, start the slide foot on board 15. The target is the second arrow. Slide to 13. For the 6-pin, 10-pin, or 6/10 spare, start the slide foot on board 10. The target is the second arrow. Slide on 14.

System Three

This is the 3-6-9 spare adjustment system. This system assumes the use of a strike ball. In order to implement this system you must know where to stand for your strike shot and your 10-pin shot. The kicker is that you depend on the lane's not changing and information about oil patterns' holding true throughout the competition. This is iffy with today's conditions.

The numbers 3, 6, and 9 refer to the number of boards to the right you move to make any left-side spares. For the 2-pin or 8-pin, move three boards to the right of your strike position and use your strike target. For the 4-pin, move six boards right. For the 7-pin, move nine boards right, still using your strike target.

For right-side spares, adjust from your 10-pin shot. Move three boards right of your 10-pin spot for the 6-pin and six boards right for the 3- or the 9-pin spare. With this method, you change the angle of the ball through the heads and at the arrows.

Some scratch players change hand positions and use a strike ball. The purpose of this method is to make the strike ball roll end over end and act like a plastic ball. This takes a higher degree of skill and practice. Using a plastic spare ball takes this complication out of play.

There are many ways to convert spares. The important thing is to gain every bit of knowledge you can about spare shooting and then don't hesitate to use any or all of that knowledge. Remember, the problem is not leaving something after the first ball. It's leaving something after the second.

Visualization

A key mechanism to aid great spare shooting is visualization. Think of visualization as a spare-shooting time machine. You stand in the present, engaged in imagining a future that has not yet occurred (Vealey 1986). You complete the spare in mind and body as if you have already succeeded. This gives you an opportunity to prove that seeing into the future is possible.

A point of clarification is called for here. We have just finished discussing the importance of staying in the present to achieve great spare shooting. Why is it OK now to discuss living in the future? Here is the distinction. The negative aspect of living in the past and future has to do with consequences, that is, thinking about the results of made or missed shots. Usually this has frustration, worry, or anger attached to it if a shot was missed. There might also be anxiety, excitement, or fear about a shot yet to be taken. In each of these cases the wonderful or difficult feelings have to do with what did, or will, happen.

A key mechanism to aid great spare shooting is visualization. Think of visualization as a spare-shooting time machine. You stand in the present, engaged in imagining a future that has not yet occurred *as if it were happening as you think about it*. In effect you are in two time zones at once—the real now and the visualized event as if it were now happening.

In visualization there is no thought about the consequences of making or missing the present, or any, shot. In a sense, visualization is timeless. Some people have said that the genius of Walt Disney was his ability to imagine the future as he designed his empire. Interviews with successful athletes from a wide variety of competitive sports have shown that as many as 98 percent of them use some form of imagery (Nideffer 1985). Again, some people confuse imagery with hoping and wishing. Although it is true that wanting to perform without taking action is merely fantasy, specific actions will lead to success on the lanes.

Visualization is a special form of imagery. It is using the mind's eye to imagine and feel something as if it were happening in the body or on the lanes.

Visualization happens all the time in daily life even outside the realm of sports. A woman who is late for an event, for example, may go through the route in her mind as a way of visualizing the most efficient path to travel. This is like trying reality on for size first, approving the plan, and then putting the imagined plan into action. A similar process can take place in setting up spares.

Most people have heard the phrases *self-fulfilling prophecy* and *seeing is believing*. Visualization is a way to breathe life into those sayings with respect to shot delivery. All bowlers have a pretty good idea of what they can and cannot accomplish. If you cannot see yourself shooting spares (or performing any other bowling skill), this may indicate a lack of mental preparedness for executing the skill. On the other hand, if you can picture and feel making the spare, you probably have a good mental setup for success.

Imagery can encompass more than just seeing in the mind's eye. This process involves internal senses: seeing, hearing, touching, and perhaps even smelling and tasting. One of the great things about using imagery is that in bowling situations so many senses are stimulated. For example, imagine yourself in competition play. You can see the approach and the shot path, feel the ball, sense your stance and movement, and hear the sounds of pins cracking.

To clarify terms, *imagery* is the involvement of any of the senses in creating a mental experience. *Visualization* is seeing through your own mind's eye the actions and results of your efforts. Don't get too hung up on these terms. Think of it like this. While utilizing imagery, you can use muscle, touch, smell, sound, and sight to imagine going through a shot sequence. Using visualization, you can see the ball travel on its path, the ball rotation and speed, and even the entry of the ball into the pins.

Follow these steps to apply imagery and visualization to making spares.

First, use a focused relaxation option. Take a moment to take a deep breath, use calming self-talk, or use conscious muscle relaxation; in general, take a break from running on automatic. Engaging in visualization is far more difficult if you do not take a break in your routine, however short. Visualization is a decision. You must be self-collected enough to apply it.

Next, see the ball's behavior in your mind. There are two places to visualize attention and focus: seeing where the ball travels on the lanes, and seeing the actual reaction of the ball. In seeing ball reaction, follow the path of the spare shot in your mind's eye. For example, imagine a trench through which the ball will travel. Another technique is to see a wide, painted stripe that illustrates the ball's path. In any event, you must have a picture of the road the ball is going to take.

Another effective visualization technique is to see the tilt and roll of the ball as it goes down the lane. You can use this technique without much attention to hand position and release. The visualization itself will cause you to organize your hand and body to create the result, provided that you have the basic skills to execute proper technique in the first place. Remember, especially on the strike shot, you roll to the break point, not to the pocket. You control direction, not result, even though you visualized the entire ball path.

After seeing the ball's behavior in your mind, experience your body's form and movements for executing the shot. It is important that you have a correct sense of what your body should do in terms of form, balance, and armswing. Getting a feel in your mind for what to experience is very powerful in cueing your body to respond for great coordinated, fluid shots. When setting up, make a decision about the body action you intend to use and finish with. Feel it. See it, if you can. Commit to making it happen.

Finally, use a cue word. Whatever imagery you use—watching the ball travel through a tube, imagining the ball running along a paint stripe, or using a complete armswing—develop a cue word or phrase that will activate this imagery. Examples include *solid at the line, tube, pose at the end, free armswing*, or any other words that positively activate you.

You now have the essential ingredients for reliable, rock-solid spare shooting. You need only plug in your favorite spare-shooting system, and away you go! Effective spare shooting requires becoming absolutely present, discarding past and future thinking. Get your intentions crystal clear. Plug in the technical map of where the ball should go, and visualize ball track and rotation. Add internal body visualization cues, and then launch your shot. Watch your spare completions skyrocket!

chapter

OVERCOMING BURNOUT

On the path of mastery of any sport or discipline, most athletes encounter the mental and emotional grinch called burnout. Burnout jumps you when you are in the middle of pushing forward toward personal and team goals. It lurks where there is repetition, stagnation, and exhaustion. Burnout can numb even the most excited bowlers. To deal with this mental game grinch, you must be able to spot the signs, recognize the symptoms, and take early action.

Burnout is the hidden undertow of the serious athlete. It sneaks up on the bowler, sucking energy, excitement, and enthusiasm, and subtly drowning competitive spirit. Ironically, burnout tends to strike those who strive the hardest for high achievement. Many athletes affected by burnout drop out of their sports or simply limp along with ever-declining performance.

Burnout vulnerability can be highest at the end of league season, during a swing on the professional tour, or after weeks and months of training. The problem is that bowlers confuse what may be a temporary condition with a fundamental change in their feelings about the game. The other problem is that burnout sometimes occurs when competition demands are still present. This can rob the bowler of feeling able to, or interested in, competing well.

Who Is at Risk?

The prime targets of burnout are bowlers who have worked hard on their games by training frequently, practicing diligently, and taking few training and competition breaks. These bowlers put great emphasis on achievement and winning. As a consequence, they often spend a lot of time around the bowling center, entering most of the available tournaments and bowling in multiple leagues. For those on the professional tour, time for breaks and recovery is limited.

Certain personality characteristics put some bowlers at higher risk than others. The first is perfectionism. Perfectionism is the personal demand that every shot and game yield the desired result. There is no room for errant shots, learning along the way, or recognizing that growth and improvement is a process. The self-talk of perfectionist bowlers is full of shoulds, musts, shouldn'ts, and supposed-tos. Perfectionism is like having a judge with scorecards in your head. Every time you roll a ball, the judge holds up a rating card, either 10.0 or 1.0—no middle scores. After a while, the internal pressure of having to get a 10.0 every time erodes energy and drive. This is coupled with striving to avoid the punishing feelings associated with failure.

The second personality trait that can put bowlers at risk is overconcern about what others think. It is difficult enough to focus and deliver in a competitive environment without directing attention outward. Bowlers who feel they must deliver for team-mates or not mess up in front of others often find their pilot light of competition fire blown out. It is natural to want to do well for the team. It is also normal to want to excel on the bowling stage. The problem occurs when playing the game for the attention, approval, or acceptance of others dominates. Being other-focused results in bowlers constantly trying to avoid messing up instead of searching for excellence.

Another personality trait associated with burnout is difficulty with assertiveness skills. Athletes who struggle with assertiveness can find it hard to get their needs met in training and competition situations. Their enthusiasm may be eroded when they push anger and irritation down instead of dealing with these feelings productively. Not directly handling feelings eventually creates problems with mood and energy.

Still other bowlers at risk for burnout are those who set goals so out of reach that they are continually frustrated and let down. Setting lofty goals is helpful and motivating. Setting goals too far out, or setting goals you are unlikely to achieve, is an invitation to burnout. Raising the bar can motivate training and improvement. Raising the bar so high that you never clear it cheats you out of the periodic reinforcement of successful goal achievement. It also erodes your belief in yourself as someone who overcomes obstacles.

Another significant personal risk factor for burnout is worrying continually about bowling performance. Anxious worry and concern always involve having one's mind in the past or future. This orientation takes its toll in useless expenditure of adrenaline and energy. Past and future fretting also prevents a bowler from enjoying and playing in the moment.

Enjoy and play in the moment!

During the professional tour, bowlers have to be especially careful to let past tournaments go out of mind. Those who don't often find themselves getting even more exhausted on the road. The other worry drain for the pros is having to make money at each tournament to pay expenses and make a living. To avoid burnout, bowlers must learn to section these issues off in other parts of the consciousness.

Finally, every athlete has to attend to personal health. No engine can run well with sugar water in the gas tank. Too many bowlers like to pretend that they don't have to follow the same rules for peak performance that other athletes follow. This illusion of invulnerability can put them at risk for not getting adequate sleep, not following the rules of proper nutrition, and not controlling the consumption of sugar and alcohol. The human mind and body are a system. If the system gets overrun physically, the mental part of the bowling machine suffers a greatly increased risk of burning out.

Signs and Symptoms

Some of the signs of burnout are fairly straightforward; others are subtle and can sneak up with little advance warning. An individual or team may perform with excellence through the early part of the season, and everyone can be in competitive shape, but something is off just a touch. It can be hard to put a finger on. Energy and excitement are down. Motivation to excel is a memory. Painful losses to less able bowlers can become more frequent.

Bowling burnout can be defined as the loss of interest and enthusiasm for bowling in someone who was once committed to the sport. Burnout is characterized by mental, emotional, or physical exhaustion. It can leave people feeling as though someone pulled the plug on the energy feeding the muscles. Shots are lackluster. The physical and mental games, once crisp, become dull. Bowlers are particularly susceptible when they have dreams and goals of winning, individually and as a team, and continually fall short of those goals.

Bowlers coming off the professional tour or in the latter half of league season sometimes exhibit burnout. If they practice at all, it is because they know they have to, not because they feel passion or excitement. They may even entertain thoughts of quitting. Irritability rises quickly to the surface when they throw an errant shot.

One person on a team who is dealing with burnout can seem to infect others who are bowling with them with their drained, sometimes pessimistic, energy and attitudes. The opposite can also happen. An enthusiastic, optimistic, and energetic teammate can buoy the whole team. Heck, you probably ought to have him or her lead off!

Do continued disappointments around competition outcomes lead to burnout, or does burnout lead to disappointment? The answer appears to be a circular dance. As mentioned, repeatedly failing to reach lofty goals can be tiring, frustrating, and draining, all cardinal features of burnout. On the other hand, burnout itself tends to lead to negative thinking, which leads to disappointing bowling. However it starts, once you detect this pattern, it is vital to interrupt it.

Bowling burnout can be hard to detect because it happens over a long time span. Burnout is different from the flash of disappointment after a poor outing or the bitter taste in your mouth after really wanting to win a tournament and falling short. Those are sharp, difficult, unpleasant reactions. What distinguishes those feelings from burnout is that they occur, then peak, then clear up. You know you don't have burnout if the feelings pass, leaving you with renewed enthusiasm to bowl. If your interest in bowling does not rejuvenate, burnout may be the culprit.

Burnout can show itself in mental, emotional, and physical ways. It can hide under all kinds of other symptoms. If you find yourself thinking negatively about the game in general, and negatively about your own game constantly, you may be suffering from burnout. Perhaps you are doubting your strike and spare shots more than usual. Once burnout has set in, your overall confidence sags. Irritability with yourself and other bowlers increases.

Other symptoms include not feeling like practicing anymore, a loss of interest in being coached or getting feedback, and feeling overwhelmed by responsibilities outside bowling. Physical breakdown might include constant overall fatigue, catching lots of colds, and feeling as though your whole immune system is overtaxed. Be aware that just as the mind and body are one system, work, relationships, and bowling life are also one big system of activities. Burnout in work or other areas in life can lead to bowling burnout and vice versa.

Figure 7.1 is a short checklist of common burnout symptoms.

Look out for a lowered interest in hanging out with teammates and bowling buddies whom you normally enjoy. Burnout can leave you feeling uninteresting as well as uninterested, particularly with respect to sharing bowling experiences.

None of these symptoms in and of themselves necessarily indicate burnout; symptoms can have different sources. The important thing is to watch out for patterns that endure over longer periods of time. Be honest about whether you have been pushing too hard with unrealistic goals and no recovery periods. Some of these symptoms also can indicate medical problems, so checking in with a physician is advised.

Loss of enthusiasm for the game   _____

Lack of interest in practicing skills   _____

Reduced experience of fun while practicing or competing   _____

Continued disappointment at not achieving goals   _____

General fatigue   _____

Ongoing mental and physical fatigue while bowling   _____

Declining confidence in various aspects of the game   _____

Pervasive irritability with self and others   _____

Physical breakdown, colds, nagging injuries   _____

Figure 7.1   Burnout symptom checklist.

Prevention

Take a good, old-fashioned look in the mirror and honestly appraise your bowling. List your personal goals, and then ask yourself if they are properly calibrated. If your expectations are too rigid, then you are placing yourself in a personal pressure cooker. Erosion of energy and enthusiasm are bound to follow. Set realistic goals. Challenge yourself, but refrain from burying yourself with suffocating goals.

Rest. Take breaks from training and competition periodically. Every organism in nature has three fundamental needs for survival: growth, maintenance, and repair. The mental psyche follows the same rules. If you are always driving hard at bowling, your mind and body will be striving to simply repair and maintain equilibrium. No healing, recovery, and enhancement of conditioning will have space to occur. There is no growth, much less fun.

No matter what activity you dive into—bowling, school, or relationships—periods of stepping away are essential for easing stress and providing perspective. Even in business environments, holidays, weekends, and sick time off are built into the system. The same rhythms apply to athletes. Needing time off is not a sign of weakness. In fact, trusting yourself enough to step back momentarily from training and competition patterns can be a sign of great strength and wisdom.

Some bowlers subscribe to the training philosophy that the more frames, games, and hours they practice, the better off they'll be. Some coaches believe this as well. If practicing 10 to 15 games is good, then 25 to 30 would be better. Not only does motor learning research go against this belief, but physical and mental breakdown can be a negative result.

Concentration is less sharp when practice involves unlimited time and games. Training can become monotonous. Practice time may change from an opportunity to an obligation. Look at a parallel example from academics. If a student is told to study for three hours, she may sit there, but her attention has plenty of time to wander. Studying goes on so long that it becomes a drag. But tell that same student she has one hour, and one hour only, to study, and her focus will sharpen. Study time becomes a privileged activity. Burnout is avoided.

No matter what the area of focus for practice—spare shooting, balance at the line, free armswing—limiting practice time and repetitions will increase attention. Ceilings on practice options increase a sense of value for the time spent. Energy remains high. Interest and excitement concerning training stay fresh.

Naturally, food, diet, and exercise come into play as well. When the rest of the machine is well taken care of, the mental, physical, and emotional components have the best chance to rest, recover, and improve. Attitudes toward physical care and well-being often reflect general attitudes about other aspects of life. Take the self-inventory about diet, exercise, rest, and recovery shown in table 7.1.

Balance in these four areas cannot be emphasized enough. Athletes in other precision, individual sports—for example, gymnasts and divers—understand this. Those athletes have a hard time performing when their bodies or mental games are not razor sharp.

Many bowlers seem to be slow in catching up to other athletes regarding a belief in the competitive advantages or good physical self-care. Bowling has a mischievous trap built into it. Bowlers can be overweight and have bad wind from smoking and still roll a powerful ball. Some of the legends of the game, past and present, were periodically heavy drinkers. We see the same thing in golf, in which individual skills can be performed despite poor conditioning.

TABLE 7.1 SELF-ASSESSMENT OF DIET, EXERCISE, RECREATION, AND REST HABITS

Evaluate your habits in each area shown on the chart by writing a mark under the heading that best characterizes your diet, exercise, recreation and fun, and rest and recovery.

	GREAT	OK	POOR
Diet			
Exercise			
Recreation and fun			
Rest and recovery			

Poor health habits influence bowlers in two primary ways. The first is the subtle energy drain that results from being out of shape. An athlete has to be in denial to think that the game is not affected by physical conditioning, particularly over long competition blocks, or over a long season. It simply takes extra effort to move when one is out of shape.

The second effect of improper diet, drugs and alcohol, and inadequate rest is on the emotional energy state. Susceptibility to fatigue, irritability, frustration, and overall lack of resilience is all part of being physically taxed. Long periods of time living and competing with inadequate fuel and recovery is another source of burnout.

The next step in identifying a state of burnout is to look at what other stresses are occurring in life in general. These external stresses can suck the energy from bowling enthusiasm if good stress management techniques are not on board. Stress management is like a sport with a particular set of skills to master. Several of these are similar to the relaxation exercises offered in chapter 4. Some of the most common and accessible include progressive muscle relaxation, deep breathing, exercise, and counseling. You might also schedule a visit with a counselor who can set you up with a good line of practice exercises.

Making changes in training styles and schedules can rejuvenate tired routines. Practice with friends. Participate in dollar pot games. Play for sodas. Get some fresh coaching perspectives. Allow for rest days between intense practice sessions. Anything that shakes off the staleness of overtraining and too much unconscious repetition can send fresh blood into a dragging season.

One note of caution: Even when playing in casual fun games, practice your shot cycle, including your preshot routine. These are great opportunities to groove in desired patterns in low-stakes environments.

One of the simplest things you can do to combat burnout is to shift perspective. Not many good things can happen when the internal critical eye is always watching. Allow all parts of your bowling to be considered a work in progress instead of demanding flawless perfection every time. In the mental world of competition tension, having to be perfect is a way of playing scared.

Demand excellence instead, which simply means opening up and giving it what you've got.

Curing Burnout

If you are fatigued at the bowling center and sick of bowling, if you are already bowling worse because your mental game has declined or you are thinking of quitting, then burnout may well be the problem. If the diagnosis fits, there are three basic intervention options.

Option 1 is to simply do nothing. Surprisingly, this seems to be a common choice. The reality is that most people keep operating within their comfort zones. This means that they deal with life by doing what is normal and usual. Without waking up and doing something different, you may be condemning yourself to a continued slide into the burnout doldrums. Some have defined insanity as doing the same thing repeatedly and expecting different results. Taking option 1, doing nothing, is leaving it up to time and hope to cure burnout. Dining on hope may leave you starving.

Some athletes quit at this point. This is a drastic measure that doesn't call for a shift in how one handles competitive life. Teammates and bowling buddies lose. You lose something you once loved. Quitting doesn't allow you to grow as an athlete. Remember that how you participate in sports often reflects your overall approach to life. Sometimes quitting is a long-term drastic solution to a short-term problem that could be effectively addressed otherwise.

Option 2 is to take a break, not a retirement. Note that taking a break, structuring some recovery time, and allowing for mental and physical healing is different from quitting. All healing occurs during downtime. Plan for time off to make room for refueling. If this is your plan, however, you should take some time to figure out what may have led to the burnout in the first place. Areas to check include overtraining, a heavy competition regimen, critical self-judgment, and continually falling short of high performance goals. Do not just rest up and go back to doing all the things that landed you in the soup in the first place. Make some conscious and committed choices about how to keep the razor sharp.

A break from bowling will give yourself time to recover from burnout. You may need to put away your bowling ball and step away from the game for a time.

Taking breaks does not necessarily mean putting away the bowling balls for extended periods of time. It can mean taking days, weeks, or tournaments off. It can also mean letting go of bowling completely when you leave the bowling center and focusing on other meaningful elements of your life.

Continuing to play through burnout can look like intense training and competition, exhaustion, staleness, more practices, more competitions, followed by a mental and emotional crash. Worse yet is continuing this burnout pattern even in the face of declining performance, bad moods, pessimism, and joylessness. This pattern is so draining it should be prevented or detected and cured at all costs.

Option 3 is to get a hand from someone who can act as a guide in this situation. Isolation is the accomplice to burnout. Find a coach, friend, family member, or sport psychologist who can help you pull back from the game for a moment. Get other points of view on what might be linked to the burnout experience. Look at the recipe checklist of risk factors shown in figure 7.2. Take a clear look at yourself to see if you exhibit any of the signs of burnout—in your thinking, goal setting, or practicing styles.

Sometimes merely airing out the experience of burnout with someone who is safe and supportive can jump-start the recovery process. Acknowledging symptoms and talking about them is like an inoculation against the virus called burnout. Some change in thinking, training, or competing patterns is going to be called for. An army of at least two on the recovery side will be helpful.

Bowling burnout is far easier to prevent than it is to cure. If you are an ambitious competitor, excited about bowling, and bent on taking the game as far as you can, make sure to protect yourself from overrunning your mental, emotional, and physical engines.

Perfectionistic thinking   _____

Intense emotional reactions that remain long after games
and tournaments are over   _____

Goals set too high or too low   _____

Limited periods of rest or recovery from practice or
competition   _____

Physical rundown and poor health maintenance routines   _____

Social isolation; few or no supportive relationships   _____

Loss of meaning in participating in the sport   _____

Pressure to have to make money competing in order
to survive   _____

Self-acceptance and self-esteem based on bowling
performance   _____

Figure 7.2 Checklist of burnout risk factors.

Set high goals and standards, but not unrealistic ones. Maintain physical conditioning, a healthy diet, and rest. Find a safe coach, counselor, or friend to debrief the daily battles of life and bowling. With these prevention arrows in the quiver, life on the lanes can remain refreshing and fun.

chapter

SLUMP BUSTING

Every serious bowler goes through ups and downs. Sometimes all goes well. Your feel for armswing, ball release, and lane play is tops. You are brimming with confidence. Maybe you even believe that you finally have this game knocked. Anyone who stays with bowling long enough will be treated to days and weeks like this. The problem is that every bowler who is on an improvement path, or even striving to maintain a level of excellence at the top of the heap, is going to be subject to the letdown experience called the *slump.*

A slump is a time period of various lengths when you feel stuck in terms of performing up to your capabilities or being able to improve your game. You may experience declining scores and confusion and wonder what is happening. Frustration goes up. Sometimes you experience a mix of self-directed anger, anxiety, and loss of interest in, or energy for, competing. You lose perspective. The slump feels like a terminal event instead of part of the competitive growth process.

When it comes to slumping bowling performance, there are two kinds of bowlers. The first kind is not very bothered. Bowlers of this type do not work on their games, accept their current skill levels, and take each league or tournament experience as a separate event. Leagues are used as practice sessions. These bowlers may have declines in performance, but because they are not actively working on improvement or top-level performance, subpar bowling doesn't necessarily send them into the doldrums that indicate a slump.

The second kind of bowler is on a path of improvement and excellence. All paths of mastery for any skill or art include steps that are dark, disheartening, or even scary. If the path is long and meaningful, there will be periods of fatigue, loss of direction, and stumbling. This chapter is about those little stutter steps and what to do about them. Of course, there are gratifying and exciting parts of the journey as well.

Athletes in every sport, including bowling, experience slumps. Bowling is a sport that requires high repetition and repeatability of basic skills. If something is off in the mental or physical game, a slump can affect the bowler; if not fixed, it can stick around for a while. Like it or not, all bowlers have good days and bad days. There are plenty of painful 130s and exciting 250s in most bowlers' lives.

One bad outing does not indicate a slump. Rather, a slump can be defined as an enduring pattern of substandard performance. Practicing and competing without being effective over a period of time can indicate a slump. Slumps have mental and emotional components. Bowlers in slumps often worry, become concerned, overanalyze, and expect continued problems in the game. Self-punishing thoughts about being a bad bowler or being stupid can appear. Feelings of frustration, anxiety, low-level depression, and anger are common during slumps. Typically, bowlers in slumps worry about how long the slump will last and whether they will be able to shake it.

Slumps are a natural part of the competition and improvement process. They are a test of both character and commitment. Slumps are an opportunity to cure something that isn't working in the overall game. They also cause the athlete to examine training habits, stress levels inside and outside of bowling, and overall burnout. Slumps can also reflect a period when training, learning, and competing are all being digested and metabolized. This can be a hidden part of one's growth as a bowler.

© Sleeping Dogs Communications

Slumps are part of competition and test a bowler's character and mettle.

The results of slumps may not be pretty. Some players quit or give up the game for a time. They lose confidence. Their enjoyment of the game plummets and the feelings from the slump can affect other parts of their lives. It does not have to be this way, though. If slumps can be recognized for what they are—part of the process—they can be brief, nondistressing, and even productive.

Identifying Slump-Producing Habits

There is a saying that time heals all wounds. Actually, time alone has never healed anything; it has only made space for healing agents to work. Although a break may sometimes clear the fog, a slump is like an athletic flu. Something is going on. It helps to identify the source of the slump and make decisions about the most appropriate actions to take.

The first thing to do when you have been bitten by the slump bug is to examine and repair self-talk. Bowlers who sink into the mire of slump negativity are often victims of "stinkin' thinkin'." The mental game approaches listed in the Diagnosis and Recovery sections of this chapter can free them from the shackles of a slump. The alternative of doing nothing, or worse engaging in the wrong things, can sentence a bowler to long periods on a slump path.

The excellence process is like a path that has subtle, sometimes hidden, obstacles. If you are really alert and know what to watch for, you can recognize the danger signs and avoid tripping into one of the slump traps. Recognition also affords the opportunity to see when a slump trap has snagged you, and to take action in freeing yourself. Watch out for the following common mental traps on the excellence and improvement path.

Mental Trap #1: Negativity About Self

Bowlers who are mentally sinking tend to see themselves in a negative light. This may not seem like an earth-shaking revelation, but slow down and consider this point. It is nothing to make a face, swear, or experience frustration about a bad shot, game, or competition block. However, bowlers who are in emotional slumps or struggling with the physical game are likely to attack themselves repeatedly. When their performances are not up to standard, they think something is fundamentally wrong with them. For example, a bowler who misses a lot of spares in a given week or month may get down on himself as a bowler, maybe even as a person, and create a negative self-image.

A negative self-image destroys confidence. It may lead to the emergence of hateful self-fulfilling prophecies. Bowlers start to question their ability to carry shots and complete spares. Their feelings of embarrassment around performance contribute to bad feelings about themselves. They may then experience pressure around bowling as they attempt to avoid the negative thoughts and feelings that come with poor bowling.

In this developing scenario, bowlers start to press and tighten to force better bowling. This further compromises the natural swing. Instead of bowling for the great feeling of executing like a champion, competitors shift focus to avoiding aversive feelings, negative thoughts about themselves, and more weak bowling.

This negative feedback loop results in a downward spiral. Negative self-evaluation leads to difficult feelings such as frustration, depression, and anger. Thoughts such as "I stink" or "I shouldn't be out there" or "I can't bowl" are common. Pressure increases to avoid these unpleasant thoughts and feelings. Muscles tighten. Shots are pointed. Scores go down. The pattern continues. Some bowlers even start to experience fear before rolling shots.

Mental Trap #2: Pessimism About Change

Bowlers who are slumping physically and emotionally tend to be pessimistic about possible help or change. When a bowler is in a slump, everything goes through the negative filter in the mind. The result is that no matter what is happening, the data is processed negatively. The bowler may have decreased faith in coaching, little confidence in the ability to perform the next time out, and a sense of helplessness that anything will make a positive difference.

In addition to focusing on their shortcomings, bowlers stuck here see outside influences in negative terms as well. Lane conditions are bad or unfair. Life itself is picking on them. Nothing can help. They are like cartoon figures with rain clouds over their heads while everyone else experiences sunshine. Even bowlers who think that they are open to assistance may really be shut down to accepting help.

Mental Trap #3: Negativity About the Future

Bowlers who are struggling often think negatively about their bowling futures. This trap makes slumps even more oppressive. In addition to difficult thoughts about bowling and about the effectiveness of intervention, these bowlers are pessimistic about things turning around in the near future. This sense of hopelessness drains energy, drive, and enthusiasm.

When falling into a slump, bowlers can become frustrated, angry, depressed, and self-punishing. They feel bad about themselves, don't know what to do, and don't see any relief on the horizon. For some bowlers, these feelings last only a few weeks. In this case, all that has been described passes through as part of life.

A true slump is defined as a pattern that becomes seen as a lasting reality to the individual. In fact it is not the bowling itself that puts the bowler in a slump. It is the way the bowler thinks about bowling skills, the game, and the possibility of bowling great in the future that defines a slump. At this point, the bowler needs to identify the slump and cure it before it becomes overwhelming.

Diagnosis

Slumpers often are hamstrung by thinking distortions. The thought patterns discussed in this section can lead directly to feeling stuck and in decreased performance. Consider the expression, *perception is reality*. In fact, these mental habits are the danger zone perceptions that lead to slumping realities. Check to see if you are prone to any of them.

All-or-None Thinking

If you are an all-or-none thinker, you view bowling in black-or-white, one-or-10 terms. You either bowl great or feel bad. Anything short of perfect performance is unacceptable. If you don't win or make the cut, then the outing is a failure. You have strong reactions to errant shots or not carrying the corner pins. The panorama of normal life that includes great, good, and weak performances is lost to you. Good and bad are the blanket descriptions for shots, games, and competition blocks.

The reality is that you are never the same bowler from day to day. Sometimes you have a feel for timing. Sometimes you can see where the shot needs to be played. Sometimes you clear the thumb more efficiently. And sometimes while one aspect of the game is strong, positive, and in the forefront of your consciousness, another part of your game has regressed.

You may feel great on some days, but even on the days that you think you are completely horrible, you are not. You are simply awake and aware of certain mental and physical aspects of good bowling, and unconscious of other aspects.

Overgeneralization

If you are an overgeneralizer, you exaggerate anything that is unsatisfactory. For example, you see one missed spare, a bad practice day, or a weak tournament as a bigger problem than it really is. You overgeneralize the nature and extent of your bowling difficulties and see your mistakes as part of a never-ending pattern. You might see two missed 10-pin spares in one outing as a general problem in spare shooting and turn it into a much bigger problem than it actually is.

When you overgeneralize, you forget the positive elements of growth, progress, and execution. You do not recognize that stumbles and falls occur on the path to mastery. Poor outings cause you to lose sight of the improvement process.

Mental Blender

When you are wedded to the mental blender, you take all the mistakes, errant shots, and physical flaws in your game and blend them into a poisonous negative milkshake. All feedback, information, and results are potential ingredients for the mental blender. Frustration, anger, or self-punishing thoughts prevent you from seeing the elements of your game that are working. Instead you scan your environment for more ingredients to add to the poisonous drink. The result is a form of overgeneralization that is fed by searching for negative evidence about your game.

Dismissing the Positive

Rather than seeking out negativity, as bowlers who are mental blender types tend to do, you may simply dismiss good shots, positive elements of overall execution, and even lucky breaks. If you suffer from this mental pattern, you forget, dismiss, or explain away the upside of the game and competition experience. In this way you find supporting evidence for your self-doubt. Dismissing the positive kills hope and sabotages the understanding that growth in bowling is a process of ups and downs like any other excellence process.

Are you the kind of bowler who scowls when others compliment you or rejects positive input? This is a sure sign that you suffer from this mental pattern. The result is similar to the result of mental-blender thinking: You are left with only the negative aspects of the game.

Jumping to Conclusions

Jumping to conclusions is another symptom of unfounded pessimistic thinking. Even without evidence, you may go right to the worst possible scenarios surrounding competition. Examples include thinking an errant shot or bad game means that your skills are declining or that you will never be able to handle certain kinds of oil patterns. Another example is when chance negative interactions or poor outings lead to fears that teammates don't like you or don't want you on the team. You seem to be just waiting to see negative things about yourself and the game. When you jump to conclusions, you use any piece of evidence to prove your negative self-theory.

Catastrophizing

Catastrophizing is like personal fortune telling. If you have this thinking style, you blow up problems and mistakes bigger than they actually are and predict that things will get worse and last a long time. You fret over aspects of your bowling, thinking that problems and mistakes mean that bad events and outcomes will continue to occur. You enter league night and tournaments with feelings of fear and pessimism. Every poor shot, game, and tournament becomes evidence of the truth of your catastrophic thoughts.

Believing in Emotions

Going with your gut feeling when making a decision is usually a good idea. During a slump or while dealing with negative emotions, however, your feelings may not be the greatest indicators of reality. The risk is that you will believe that frustration, depression, boredom, or anger signals truths about negative aspects of yourself, or the chances of improving and breaking out of the slump. Emotions are very powerful aspects of the mental game. Negative thinking habits tend to lead to powerful, difficult feelings. The feelings then incorrectly serve as further evidence of whatever thinking habit you are using.

Shoulding

When self-talk includes the words *should, shouldn't, must, mustn't,* and *have to,* trouble can be on board. This is the language of perfectionism that leads to guilt, frustration, and self-directed anger. When you believe you are supposed to strike every time, pick up every spare, and never throw errant shots, you are setting yourself up for a guaranteed letdown.

Perfectionist thinking is exhausting. It also leaves you feeling perpetually inadequate. If you are not already in a slump, then *shoulding* will help to create one.

Labeling

Labeling occurs when you use one or two words to describe yourself, your ability, or your bowling. It is a way of overgeneralizing that leaves out details that would provide a balanced perspective. Calling yourself a failure, saying "I'm terrible," stating that your bowling stinks, or declaring that your bowling sank the team are all ways of wrapping up a whole self-judgment in a word or statement. This is another way of viewing only the negative parts of experience. If you believe yourself, it takes only a few repetitions of labeling to land you in a slump.

If you recognize yourself in two or more of these thinking styles, you are at risk for the kind of mental pressure that leads to slumps. Remember, perception is reality. Athletes are anchored in their thinking and experience by the self-talk they employ. The good news is that knowing that self-talk creates reality is one of the keys to breaking free of the chains of stinkin' thinkin'.

Recovery

Some bowlers are able to pull out of slumps after only a few weeks. Others are more entrenched and may benefit from some effective intervention techniques. Luckily, a number of slump-busting and mood-stabilizing approaches are available. The most important point, however, is to do something! Here is a five-step approach for curing slump-bound thinking patterns:

1. Identify self-talk.
2. Observe feelings caused by self-talk.
3. Change self-talk.
4. Observe changes in thoughts and feelings caused by the new self-talk.
5. Review the new self-talk and practice it.

Write down your thoughts at each step so you have a record of what you are thinking and how you are acting to bust the slump. Likely, you will observe desirable changes in execution following effective implementation of these steps.

Step 1 is to identify self-talk. If you know that you are contending with prolonged frustration, loss of confidence, or declining energy and enthusiasm, you have likely fallen prey to one of the eight thinking patterns listed earlier. Read through them again and make a self-diagnosis. If you cannot see it in yourself, ask someone close to you. They may have observed one or more of these patterns when you talk about yourself or your bowling experience.

Step 2 is to notice and state what feelings result from self-talk. The words you use to describe yourself and your experience tend to determine your feelings. Feelings tacked on to negative thoughts are what make slumps so difficult. Frustration, irritation, depression, anger, and hopelessness are some of the most common feelings that accompany slumps. Battling feelings can have a profound impact on your ability to relax, focus, free up your armswing, and stay aware of other aspects of the physical game. It's time to change all that.

Step 3 is to change self-talk. At the very least this will allow for a truer, less distorted experience of the process of competing and improving. Look again at the thinking patterns that apply to you. Start by sifting out all-or-none statements. Instead of statements such as, "I always stink," "I'll never get better," "Nothing I do makes a difference," or "I was terrible," modify your language. Adaptive self-talk can take many forms depending on what has happened. Here are some sample positive self-talk statements:

- "Shake it off. Every shot is a new moment in time."
- "Everyone has an errant shot (or game) periodically."
- "Focus. Make a good shot."
- "Just because I don't have the good feeling today does not mean I can't bowl."
- "Getting better is a process. I won't always have my A-game."
- "Let me attend to the aspects of the game that I am doing well."

Any phrase or idea that avoids all-or-none thinking or that makes room for positive aspects of experience is a good way to direct your thinking.

Look at reality. Bowling and skill development is a process. Nothing about you or your bowling can be accurately described in black-and-white, all-or-nothing terms. You can acknowledge that you didn't care for the results, but stay away from extreme statements. Anything described in absolute terms is not going to help you and probably isn't true. If nothing else, you can compliment yourself on effort, commitment, and being on the field of battle instead of just spectating.

Step 4 is to notice whether your feelings about yourself, the game, and the competition process varied with the change in self-talk. If you have done a rigorous job of examining and changing self-talk, then thoughts and feelings about yourself and being in a process instead of a slump will also change. The result is often a positive shift in physical execution.

Changing self-talk must not be a con job. You have to see an actual positive shift in how you think about yourself and your bowling. You cannot simply say affirmations and expect to feel better. When you change self-talk, the new statement has to be real and true. If your thoughts and feelings have not changed, it is probably because you are not applying yourself wholeheartedly or don't believe in the new point of view. Sometimes it is useful to have someone else help you develop alternative ways of looking at the bowling experience. You may have to go back and repeat the steps. Just like developing other skills, walking through this process takes practice before it becomes effortless.

Step 5 is to review and practice. If you are still stuck in negative thoughts and feelings, take another run through the steps. Consider having someone help you. Make sure you write down the thoughts and feelings at each step. This will ensure that you are following the process properly, and that you are tracking your thoughts. Write down self-talk thoughts, feelings, and beliefs; self-talk challenges; new feelings and beliefs; and review and practice notes. The proof is in the pudding. If this technique works for you, you will likely see actual performance shifts in how you free up your bowling.

Bleacher-Seat Vision

Often people simply advise a bowler to wait for the slump to subside, as though it were a weather pattern that came with the wind and will leave on its own. Slumps happen for a variety of reasons, but they are not random events that occur because of bad luck. Unless you discover the contributing factors, you may not be able to stump your slump. Self-talk was reviewed in the last section. Now it is time to introduce the eye in the sky called feedback.

Many people do not distinguish between feedback and criticism. Others define criticism as negative reflections and feedback as positive reflections. Feedback in its purest form, however, is nonjudgmental information about the subject.

The most familiar feedback generators are tape recorders and video cameras. Despite your reactions to hearing or seeing a recording of yourself, neither machine uses judgment. The tape and video recorders do not suggest that you should sound like Frank Sinatra or Barbara Streisand or that you should lose weight and tone up. The video camera does not say that your bowling is good or bad. Machines are pure reporters. They simply generate feedback.

Criticism, on the other hand, always carries a should or a shouldn't with it. Criticism thrives on perfectionist thinking. It paints you as good or bad. Either way, it is judgmental.

Many bowlers get mad at the pins when they are not happy with their results. The pins, however, are the perfect feedback generators. Overall, the pins tell you how well you are rolling the ball, whether you have made the right ball and surface choice, and whether you are bowling on the right line. The pins don't mock you, praise you, or criticize you. They are pure feedback about bowling effectiveness.

If you are camped in a slump, feedback from outside sources may be essential to help you make decisions about what to change. Your only other option is to draw from your own thinking processes, which, as we have seen previously, may be far from helpful at this point. You have already tried everything available from the inside out. Getting a view from the outside in is the next option.

There are several ways to obtain an outside-in point of view. One is to pretend you are viewing yourself from the spectators' position. Imagine every part of the approach and delivery. Is your armswing free? Are you staying down and balanced at the line? Are you grabbing the ball? These are the sorts of questions to ask and answer. It is helpful to have a checklist of physical and mental game elements that you can scan for performance cues (see figure 8.1). Better yet, get a video camera and zero in on your approach and delivery. Indisputable visual evidence is a powerful tool for diagnosing and treating the physical parts of a slumping game. The best tool of all is a trustworthy, knowledgeable coach who knows how to communicate with you effectively.

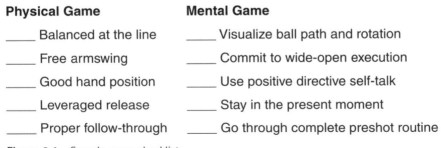

Physical Game

_____ Balanced at the line

_____ Free armswing

_____ Good hand position

_____ Leveraged release

_____ Proper follow-through

Mental Game

_____ Visualize ball path and rotation

_____ Commit to wide-open execution

_____ Use positive directive self-talk

_____ Stay in the present moment

_____ Go through complete preshot routine

Figure 8.1 Sample game checklist.

You are responsible for developing your own checklist. Write down all of the important elements, and ask your coach for feedback on what you might be missing. Bring the list to practice and make sure you cover all the elements. Add elements as your awareness grows. Bringing the list to tournaments may provide a backup cueing system if your game seems to be off and you can't pinpoint what is going on.

The best physical intervention is to invite someone who can really see and understand your game to observe what is happening. A good coach is someone who can understand where you want to go, can see what is getting in your way, and can communicate effectively what he or she observes. A good coach can paint a picture of how you bowl. Effective coaching is like being able to observe yourself from the seats. Finally, a good coach can talk to you without leaving you feeling put down for not having it all together all the time.

To me, coaching is a relationship in which the athlete suspends belief in what is right about her own game play for a few moments. Instead, she places confidence in the input of a trusted observer. Coaching works when the athlete can integrate the coach's suggestions and ultimately change the way she executes skills.

One of the most difficult things to do as a bowler is to listen to feedback nonjudgmentally and use it to change things that are either outside one's awareness or outside one's comfort zone. Bowlers seem to be naturally drawn to doing what is familiar to them. It can be quite challenging to think or move in an unusual way, or to consciously perform a skill differently.

Some bowlers can hear, integrate, and make use of feedback. Others are too closed minded or proud to open themselves to outside input. Being coached is an art. Are you open to feedback? That would be the most important question to resolve in breaking free from a slump, as well as in moving forward in your overall excellence and improvement process.

Strive to be open to doing something different. Imagine that you are trapped in a raging river, about to be pulled under. Would you rather keep your hands on a log in the river instead of releasing them to reach for someone else's helping hand? The risk of letting go of comfortable or familiar ways of thinking, and executing shots, may be required to break free of habits and techniques that are binding you to a slump.

Perfection Versus Excellence

Let's go back to a concept introduced earlier in this chapter. Those who suffer slumps often fall prey to perfectionist thinking. Perfectionism breeds self-criticism, hyper-awareness of flaws and errors, and personal demands of winning and striking every time. It leaves no room for human factors. The stinkin' thinkin' traps identified earlier are all about perfectionism. Any shoulds, shouldn'ts, musts, and mustn'ts are usually reflections of perfectionism, which causes frustration and self-condemnation. Many bowlers experience slumps because they think they are not supposed to go through the normal learning curves. These slumps are total mental creations born out of unrealistic personal demands for performance. In a nutshell, perfectionism creates the psychological hell that is the slump.

Every competitive bowler has a choice: perfection or excellence. Excellence is marked by intention and commitment, not by perfect results. Excellence recognizes that any journey includes exploration, pitfalls, and successes, and that growth is a process. Athletes with an excellence orientation see learning plateaus as part of the growth curve; they do not deteriorate into slumps.

Excellence is human. Perfectionism is robotic. Excellence involves learning. Perfectionism demands first-place, strike-every-time, inhuman bowling.

Here is an illustration of how your motivation differs depending on whether you have adopted an excellence or perfectionist perspective. Imagine that there is a golden ring hanging out over the middle of a big pit. Your desire is to leap and grab the ring, which can bring you honor and wealth. Perfectionists have two accompanying thoughts. The first is an awareness of the stakes involved in making the grab. The second is to avoid missing and the punishing thoughts associated with it. In effect, the perfectionist grabs to avoid the pain of falling or losing the prize.

A player committed to excellence leaps for the ring with total commitment, heart, and intention. Fear of falling is not a consideration because the player knows it is an illusion. The value of the experience is in bringing everything possible to the effort. Continual effort and intention are the essential ingredients in a

Commit to bowling with excellence, bringing heart and intention to every shot.

process that is ongoing until the end of the player's involvement in the sport. In excellence, a slice of heaven on earth is the feeling of flight during the leap for the ring.

Few bowlers are either purely perfectionists or purely "excellentists." In pure perfectionism, every shot must be just right every time and every game. A miss brings feelings of anger, frustration, rage, or embarrassment. There may be good feelings when shots are made, but the internal judge is always working. Bowlers who have an excellence orientation are like artists always seeking to improve the stroke. The search is for the experience of greatness, not because the ego demands it, but because it naturally feels great to master anything. Feelings of joy, pleasure, warmth, and excitement go with excellence. Execution with heart is the turn-on from this perspective. All of us exhibit characteristics of both perfectionists and excellentists.

Table 8.1 compares slump-bound perfectionism with an excellence-oriented process.

Figure 8.2 shows a continuum line with excellence and growth on one end and perfectionism and slumping on the other. Where are you on the line?

To be a champion, you can perform several slump-busting, forward-moving mental game shifts. Observe the following principles.

Every thought and reaction while bowling is a choice. You can take a perfectionist view and be self-demanding, or you can opt for excellence. Each shot and game can be cursed or celebrated; each game, practice, and delivery can be understood as a step on a long, progressive path to greatness. From this point of view all slumps are still part of the path to excellence.

Perfectionism – Excellence
(prone to slumps)   (prone to growth)

Figure 8.2   Are you closer to perfectionism or excellence? Put an X where you think you fit on the line. Ask two people who know you where they see you on the continuum. Always try to move toward excellence and growth.

TABLE 8.1 COMPARISON OF PERFECTIONISTIC BOWLING AND EXCELLENCE BOWLING

Perfectionism	Excellence
Must bowl great in order to feel OK	Always brings the best to every game and shot and feels good about committed effort; pin fall is a bonus
Feels increasing pressure as the stakes get higher	Feels increased energy and excitement when the stakes get higher
Is self-critical and punishing after an errant shot or a weak game	Reviews play in order to learn and make corrections; irritation is fleeting
Is triumphant when striking; angry or enraged when missing	Ties joy to bringing best effort
Has fun only when winning	Frequently has fun while bowling
Worries when not winning or scoring	Understands that everything is part of the growth and improvement process; does not worry about stutter steps along the way
Ties ecstacies and agonies to good and bad shots and games, wins and losses	Keeps correcting and improving through the ups and downs of bowling; has both passion and perspective
Has to win; believes that winning and losing define who he/she is	Thoroughly enjoys the competition experience and rings out the joy of winning; naturally wins and improves by focusing on the process
Chokes based on pressure	Makes mistakes based on being human
Lives and dies by wins and losses	Sees winning and losing as part of a much bigger picture
Expertise	Mastery
Demands that choices and guesses be right every time	Is willing to explore new methods, techniques, and strategies
Learns by trial and error, which creates fear of failure	Takes risks in order to facilitate learning, growth, and ultimate success
Has feelings of frustration and anger	Has feelings of mastery, power, and well-being
Need for control limits discovery	Is creative and spontaneous
Judges based on individual shots, games, and tournaments	Accepts all aspects of the growth, learning, and improvement process
Is drained of energy	Is energetic and excited
Has constant doubts	Plays in an uninhibited way; shots just flow
Looks only at whether or not perfection has happened	Sees all of bowling and life as a learning, improvement process

The point of view you adopt—perfectionism or excellence—leads directly to either slumping and excessive pressure or growth and fulfillment. Remember that emotions stem from thoughts. Slumps are situations created by thought and practice patterns. The negative emotions that result are what make slumps such a drag. Reorienting your perspective will clear the feelings, which will lead to a way out.

Make the distinction between being complete and being perfect. Being flawless means bringing everything to bear that you have learned in the mental and physical game. Do your best. Participate wholeheartedly and with wild abandon. There is room for humanness there. Perfectionism, on the other hand, will not make you a better bowler.

If you are bowling in a way that you do not care for, shift something. Have the courage to seek honest feedback from others and from yourself. Take the risk of integrating the feedback and doing something different. If nothing changes in your approach to bowling, nothing changes in the results. I have never seen a great athlete who can get along without any coaching, feedback, or input. If you are slumping, get help to shorten the amount of time you hang out in the doldrums.

Take responsibility for everything that occurs in your bowling. Slumps happen to people who see themselves as victims of circumstances. The path of mastery demands that you take ownership of all your consequences and results. This perspective allows for shifts in awareness and learning. The alternative is to keep trying to fix outside conditions such as lane oil, noise, and balls instead of mastering the game.

Slump-bound thinking is like walking a balance beam. Every step is work. You have to be so careful about where you put your feet. By contrast, excellence is like walking on Main Street. When you overscrutinize, you feel as though you are stuck or going backward. The trick is to step back, see the big picture, and understand the overall process. With intention and positive practice techniques, growth is inevitable. In fact, the only thing that seems certain in the universe is that everything changes. By busting your slump, you're just speeding things up a bit.

All bowlers have games and tournaments in which they feel that a tire has gone flat or even that the wheels are coming off the car. Integrating feedback, practicing effective mental strategies, and shifting perspective from perfectionism to mastery provide freedom from the chains of slumps.

chapter

9

PRACTICE AND TRAINING

Each individual comes into the world with natural talents and abilities. At the beginning, these talents are untapped and undeveloped. Think of the scores of people written off by their parents, teachers, and coaches who have become great champions in their own rights. For example, Albert Einstein was called a slow learner. Abraham Lincoln grew up in poverty. Thomas Edison had more than 2,000 trials before finally getting his lightbulb to work. Edison had a great point of view about the practice process. He said that he never failed. There were simply a lot of steps in the process.

No babies are predestined to curl their little fingers around a bowling ball, not even the sons and daughters of bowling legends. Regardless of how natural an athlete someone is, without practice in the physical and mental aspect of games, that athlete will stay only at the level of skill that basic athleticism allows and will not get appreciably better.

The limits to how far any individual can go are unknown. No one can be considered out of the range of significant improvement or even champion status. Champions are not selected based on DNA testing, strength tests, or balance tests. Until we can measure the breadth and depth of someone's heart, no one should be kicked out of consideration. The formula for improving and winning does not rule out those who are not blessed with genetic gifts, or rule in those who are physically blessed with inborn strength and talent.

A myth of sports is that whoever wants it the most will be the champion. I don't believe this is true. Throughout the professional tour season, I talk to plenty of bowlers who deeply want and hope to win, but do not get the results for which they long. The same is true for players in leagues and local tournaments. I have also known Olympic-caliber athletes who did not develop into the world-class players they could have been. Only those with true intention who are willing to step beyond comfort zones get to scale to the top of their personal and professional mountains.

Practice, when approached correctly, is the road to ultimate goal achievement. The keys to success covered in this chapter will unlock success in bowling, work, and relationships. In fact, if anything in this chapter does not appear to apply to all three of these areas of life, then that factor is probably misunderstood or deserves to be questioned. Maximally effective practice will result in long-term improvement and championship possibilities when it includes three essential components: proper physical and mental focus, coachability, and a commitment to excellence.

Mastery

To master anything you must do the right things over and over. Then, when you think that you have it down, you must keep doing the right things over and over again. If you keep doing the right things long enough, insights about executing at the highest levels can open up for you. Be aware, however, that going down to the bowling center on league night or simply rolling practice games or pot matches is not enough. If you do not bowl with a plan and know what you have to work on, then you leave far too much to chance.

When athletes set out to achieve competition and skill goals, one of two things occurs. They either meet their goals or they start making up stories and reasons for falling short. Simply put, athletes have either results or stories.

Once you have declared any kind of bowling goal, whether it is a raised average, a tournament victory, or a spare completion, you either meet it or you don't. People rarely have much to say about achieving exactly what they declared they would achieve. The results speak for themselves.

If, for whatever reason, you miss the declared goal, the stories begin. "The lanes were hooking out of the house." "I didn't have the right equipment." "Everyone on my pair was so negative." "I just couldn't motivate myself to train." "Must have been a bad rack." "With the way they oil on league night, no one could score." "I was too tired to hold it together for the whole tournament." These are just a sampling of the kinds of things heard around bowling centers. Are these and other stories true? Maybe. They are still just stories.

It is a rare bowler who can simply either achieve the goal or take responsibility for coming up short—no excuses, stories, or rationalizations. This may sound harsh, but until you own all of it—the good, the bad, and the ugly—you will not fully realize the mastery of the mental and physical game. "I did it" or "I did not

A bowler who has achieved mastery approaches the game with intention and commitment.

do it" are the only answers. After that, it is fine to look for the reasons you did not succeed. Generally the ultimate answer will be that you lacked complete intention and commitment as noted in earlier chapters.

Bowlers often declare their intentions to improve their averages, spare shooting, and tournament results. Practice in the mental and physical games must be part of the plan to reach those goals. One problem for bowlers who commit to improvement is that they don't change practice patterns; instead they do what is already comfortable and familiar. They practice only the things that have led to the current skill and success level without adding or changing important training elements.

The following brief autobiography by Portia Nelson is a great short story that illustrates the pitfalls and potential gains of bowlers in training. See if you can translate it into your own training and competition history.

An Autobiography in Five Short Chapters by Portia Nelson

Chapter 1

I walk down the street. There is a deep hole in the sidewalk. I fall in. I am lost . . . I am helpless. It isn't my fault. It takes forever to find a way out.

Chapter 2

I walk down the same street. There is a deep hole in the sidewalk. I pretend I don't see it. I fall in again. I can't believe I am in the same place. But it isn't my fault. It still takes a long time to get out.

Chapter 3

I walk down the same street. There is a deep hole in the sidewalk. I see it is there. I still fall in. It's a habit. My eyes are open. I know where I am. It is my fault. I get out immediately.

Chapter 4

I walk down the same street. There is a deep hole in the sidewalk. I walk around it.

Chapter 5

I walk down another street.

Adapted, by permission, from Portia Nelson, *There's a hole in my sidewalk: The romance of self-discovery* (Hillsboro, OR: Beyond Words Publishing).

In many ways, this is a classic story of the practice and competition life of many bowlers. In chapter 1, you are lost in the common and normal patterns of thought and skill execution. This is typical when you are in a slump (see chapter 8). This also occurs when you practice with no coaching, feedback, or other input. There are "holes" in everyone's game. Without taking responsibility for identifying these holes, feelings of helplessness are inevitable.

This chapter also applies to resistance to adapting to oil changes on the lanes, using different balls, and learning versatile hand positions. Without a commitment to do something differently, you are sentenced to repeat the sweet, bitter, and bittersweet parts of the game forever.

Chapter 2 in the bowler's autobiography is about the phenomenon of denial. Denial is what happens when you are aware of the truth but feel it is easier to pretend that something else is real. The most basic form of denial is taking a passive victim perspective, ignoring the fact that you really are responsible for what is happening in the game. This is particularly evident when you resort to blaming external or internal factors for your failure to excel. You may target external factors such as lane conditions or ball drillings or internal factors such as age, ability, and personality. The longer it takes for you to take responsibility for making changes in the mental and physical game, the longer it will be before positive results can appear.

In this part of the story you know that something is not working, but you keep on doing the same thing, hoping for different results. Insight and skill development are not likely to occur by simple repetition in practice. On the contrary, incorrect form and technique may be grooved into muscle memory instead.

Waking up and starting to get honest are the hallmarks of chapter 3. You become aware of habits and tendencies that are hindering your progress or hurting your game. At this stage, you begin to acknowledge negative, limiting mental and physical behaviors as they occur. With coaching and feedback, you have the chance to employ new skills. You take responsibility for what is, and is not, working in practice and competition.

In chapter 4, you begin to recognize external circumstances such as lane conditions, competitors, and equipment, as well as personal skills and attributes. You have a personal tool chest of acquired talent and resources. At this stage, you are able to recognize and handle your problems. You seek appropriate coaching and consultation. Most athletes think that this is the top of the mountain—problem recognition, intervention, and then positive solution. However, this is not the end of the journey.

Chapter 5 embodies the elements of true mastery. The preference is to deal with new challenges instead of the drudgery of the old and familiar. At this stage you do not fall for the trap doors that have appeared over time in the mental and physical game. Instead you adapt. You do not rest on current skill development because you understand that growth, improvement, and a deeper understanding of the game are part of bowling life.

In this chapter of your bowling life you recognize the signs that changes are needed before problems develop. You identify past missteps and aggressively pursue coaching and feedback. In competition, you have no preconceived ideas about how to play the lanes or which balls to use. You are able to process information about lane play in the moment. Before the stakes become too high, you handle pressure to avoid its becoming a problem.

Operating at this level does not mean that you are finished growing. It simply means that you are open to exploring new styles, hand positions, equipment, mental focus techniques, and other aspects of the game. In the end, there are two kinds of bowlers: those who act like victims of the game's circumstances and those who take responsibility for seeing the truth of how they bowl and what they need to practice to continually get better.

The choice is always there. How quickly you progress from chapter 1 to chapter 5 is your choice. What chapter are you in right now? To improve your mental and physical game skills, you must first do things right in practice, even if it means leaving the common and usual path behind.

Practice for Maximum Improvement

Practice for mastery of any sport has essential requirements. It is not enough to simply log hours on the lanes and repeat key physical moves. In fact, this can be harmful. Training carelessly, or only working on what feels fun and comfortable, can groove some bad habits.

Being lazy about practice intentions can leave you in chapters 1 and 2 of the bowler's autobiography—repeating mistakes and weaknesses in your game and pretending that what you are doing will improve you. The practice elements described in this section are designed to propel your game to ever-higher levels. Remember that all elements of practice can be transferred to competition as needed.

Whether you are a touring professional or a dedicated league bowler, the first critical element of practice is to set a specific goal for the day. Far too often bowlers go down to the bowling center just to see how they are rolling the ball that day or to roll for high scores. Decide which parts of the mental and physical game you will attend to. Decide how you will determine the success of the day. Without setting specific goals, you have no way to measure accomplishments. Merely logging time on the lanes is not enough. Hand positions, balance, focus, thumb release, and recovering and resetting for fresh shots are all examples of practice goals. The list is endless.

A great resource for goal setting can be found in your self-evaluation from chapter 1. Although there is value in strengthening your strengths, you will make your most significant gains in the areas you know to be your weaknesses. Self-evaluation, personal goals, and practice focus are clearly related. Goal setting is the gas in the motivation engine. Be clear about where you are going, what you will work on, and whether your area of attention will serve your bowling mission.

When practice is over, be honest with yourself. What goals did you meet and what areas need attention at your next practice? To be rigorous with goal achievement, keep a log in which you record practice goals. Be sure to record both successes and failures. Embracing true results will provide the necessary feedback for tracking growth and progress.

In Japanese martial arts there is a process called *mokso* at the beginning and end of the workout. *Mokso* is a moment in which all of the students stop to clear their minds of external concerns and pressures. This is the time they commit to being completely present for the training session at hand. Martial artists understand that if they bypass these moments, they sacrifice maximum training benefits. In addition, if trainees are not completely mentally present in practice, someone might get hurt.

Fortunately, the risk of injury is quite a bit lower in bowling. Unfortunately, the lack of dire consequences keeps many bowlers from getting themselves completely clear and mentally present for practice. Don't just drive to the bowling center, unload the equipment, put your shoes on, and start bowling. Stop for a moment. Commit to being and staying aware throughout the practice session. Decide what areas to focus on during that time.

When practice is over, stop for a moment. Prepare mentally to return to the outside world. In so doing you make a clear distinction between being *on* in terms of practice and competition focus and being formally *off.* Operating at this level of intention will generate a sense of mastery that translates to competition and to the action and recovery phases of the shot cycle. This procedure is easy to take to any bowling center or tournament in the world. Later, you can use it to center and normalize yourself, particularly in high-tension situations.

Remember, there are no throwaway shots or moments in practice. A commitment to excellence demands that every moment be an opportunity to prepare for the next shot, decide how to work on the game, or reflect on what happened the last turn. Ideally, once practice starts, everything you do in the bowling center is practice for everything you intend to do in competition. Certainly there can be downtime between turns, with lots of laughs included, but this should be a conscious choice, not a matter of simple habit. Better to have a time-limited practice with exquisite intentions than to throw a lot of shots and games without working on improvement.

Do in practice what you intend to do in tournaments. Practice is reflected in competition. Go through your preshot routines, take time between shots, and prepare for careful spare shooting as part of practice. Emotional expression and control also should be included.

In practice, you should also keep an eye out for pacing problems. Bowlers in training face two types of pacing issues. The first is rapid-fire shot throwing during practice, in which they simply grab balls off the ball return and roll shots without stopping to reflect on what just happened and what will be the area of focus for the next shot. When you practice like this, speed picks up. Emotional reactions are unchecked. Shots are wasted, and you risk grooving in bad habits. Bowling faster and faster without pause or reflection will result in improper technique, exhausted arms, sloppy focus, and lack of rewarding experience.

The other pacing issue facing bowlers in training is learning the difference between rhythm in practice and rhythm in competition. It is a far different experience to sit, wait, think, and then have a turn in league or tournament play, than it is to stand at the ball return and stay in motion, as many bowlers do in practice. To solve this problem, retreat off the approach after each shot. Do not stay by the ball return. Each practice shot should be a model of what to do in competition. Use your established preshot routine, which should contain a brief reflection on the last shot, a decision about what area to focus on for the next shot, and execution. This process slows time down to the present moment. In short, you should try to use your optimal shot cycle in every situation.

Having a training partner helps maintain competition rhythm and patterns. Getting into low-stakes or mock competitions with training partners also provides great league and tournament training conditions. This will normalize rhythm, patterns, preshot routines, focus, and pressure variables; it will also help generate enduring confidence.

Make use of imagery during practice as well. Visualize ball path, ball speed, and ball tilt. Add any other elements that you observe. If you are a good visualizer, have a picture of your own body position from the inside out. Imagine successful skill execution. What you can see in your mind you can work to manifest physically. Add the body sensations you intend to have. It's like being able to predict the future. See it. Feel it. Be it. Do it! This is similar to computer programming. The computer is your mind. Make sure that the data input is what you want. If you are not careful, you will program lazy habits instead.

Remember that there is a point in the execution sequence when you must let everything go. Thinking and preparing are done up front. Once the preshot routine is in gear, adopt one key thought and let yourself get into flow.

After each shot, game, and practice, ask yourself three questions: What worked about my execution (mental and physical)? What did not work? What will I commit to the very next chance I get? Honest answers to these questions will propel you to mastery.

The essential mental stance for any kind of success is nonjudgmental acceptance. If you approach practice from a perfectionist point of view, you will have difficulty attempting new skills, different approaches, or any changes to your game. Athletes tend to gravitate to familiar patterns. If skill development is the order of the day, then some departure from the "been there, done that" way of doing things is mandatory. To move forward, you must make acceptance of the process of experimentation part of the package. This requires a willingness to stumble along the way. Trust the process of improvement far more than the results of any given practice, tournament, or shot.

Being Coachable

Being coached requires a willingness to allow someone else's input to override your own point of view. Although this may seem simple, integrating feedback from other people can be quite challenging. Some people are natural athletes, some are natural teachers, and some are great at being coached. This section looks at improving your game through instruction.

The first step is to acknowledge that there are limits to how much your game can improve without coaching or feedback. Simple feedback comes in three basic forms: observation of ball reaction and pin fall, videotapes of yourself in action, and comments from others. One thing is certain: Without attention and adjustment to feedback, your game will not improve appreciably.

The second step in becoming a coachable athlete is a willingness to honestly evaluate the strengths and weaknesses of your current game. This can be challenging. It can be like turning bright lights on in the bathroom and really looking at your face,

Being coachable means pushing aside your point of view in order to learn from someone else's observations and experiences.

blemishes and all. True examination can be humbling, and it is essential. The only way to really do this is to get your ego out of the way for a moment and let someone else lead you.

It is much more enjoyable to look only at the things you do well. Consider this example from weightlifting. A spotter assisting a weightlifter has to decide how much weight to carry to aid the lifter. If the spotter carries a heavier load, the lifter can press more weight and perform more repetitions, increasing confidence. However, the lifter may not get as strong and may not develop a realistic picture of how much he can actually lift. Similarly, bowlers cannot know where they stand with any part of the game without clear and true feedback.

There is a saying in bowling: Trust is a must or your game is a bust. To benefit from feedback, you have to have confidence that the information is real and true and have faith in the person providing it. If you trust the person providing the feedback, then you have to surrender completely to the feedback itself. If nothing changes—for example, you just nod your head and keep doing the same things—then your game stays mired right where it is.

It is natural for teammates, friends, and teachers to want you to feel good and have a sense of accomplishment. It is just as natural to want to believe that you are making substantial improvement. It is vital that you and your coach do not collaborate to avoid facing reality. If your coach has the skill and the courage to present valuable and true feedback, and you have the spine to really look at the blemishes in your game, then great things can happen.

Take a Break

Some bowlers are so dedicated that it is hard to pull them out of the bowling center or get them to take recovery days between hard or intense workouts. Discipline and commitment to practice is certainly admirable and part of the road to success; however, sometimes desire can negatively impact physical endurance and sabotage recovery.

Research supports the value of *periodization*. The periodization model breaks training into episodes of intense, focused practice followed by rest and recovery. In the old days, athletes would train and train until they were exhausted and then repeat the cycle. This can result in mental and physical breakdown or burnout (see chapter 7). Athletes who train like this risk staleness, loss of energy and focus, and physical injury.

Most people are aware that muscles need rest and recovery. The mind also needs time to recuperate and integrate what it has learned. If you have any doubts about this, try to go without sleep. After a while, sleeping and dreaming become more compelling than food and water. The brain needs breaks too.

Keep practices sharp and time limited. Include physical recovery time. Don't be afraid to quit after 3, 5, or 10 games. If you are a bowl-a-holic, don't be shy about taking days off. Just be sure that when you show up at the bowling center, you bring all that you have.

Competitive bowlers fantasize about how well they will bowl and the improvements they will make in their games. In the end, there are no shortcuts on the path to mastery. Consider two bowlers who train at the best bowling camp in the world with the finest instruction and video feedback analysis. After camp, one bowler expects to hang on to the new skills, insights, and motivation without any changes in effort. The other plans to practice the skills and disciplines associated with long-term growth and success. Which bowler do you think will succeed? Which bowler will you choose to be?

Bowling mastery, growth, and mental game development are like a rubber band. As long as you stay with it, the rubber band expands. If you become lazy or stop attending to personal mastery, then the rubber band will begin to contract to its original form. The good news is that if you stretch it long and consistently enough, the rubber band that is your mental game never goes all the way back to its original contracted size.

The same thing will apply to readers of this book. After finishing this book, some will go back to what was comfortable and familiar before they read it. Others will venture outside their comfort zones over and over again until they master new mental game skills. This means braving frustration and risk and having trust in the overall process of excellence. It won't be an easy journey, but the destination—improved scores, higher confidence, more wins—will be worth every minute!

references
and sources

Burns, David. 1999. *Feeling good: The new mood therapy.* New York: Avon.

Davis, Martha, Elizabeth Robbins Eshelman, and Matthew McKay. 1995. *The relaxation and stress reduction workbook.* New York: MJF Books.

Gould, Daniel. 1986. Goal setting for peak performance. In *Applied sport psychology* by Jean Williams (ed.). Palo Alto: Mayfield Publishing Co.

Klemmer, Brian. 2000. *If how-to's were enough we would all be skinny, rich, and happy.* Brian Klemmer.

Kubistant, Tom. 1986. *Performing Your Best.* Champaign, Ill.: Life Enhancement Publications.

May, Jerry R., and Michael J. Asken (eds.). 1987. *Sport psychology: The psychological health of the athlete.* New York: PMA Publishing.

Millman, Dan. 1984. *Way of the peaceful warrior.* Berkeley, Calif.: Publishers' Group West.

Millman, Dan. 1999. *Body mind mastery.* Novato, CA: New World Library.

Murphy, Shane. 1996. *The achievement zone.* New York: Putnam.

Nideffer, Robert. 1985. *Athletes' guide to mental training.* Champaign, Ill.: Human Kinetics.

Orlick, Terry. 1980. *In pursuit of excellence.* Champaign, Ill.: Leisure Press.

Porter, Kay, and Judy Foster. 1986. *The mental athlete.* Dubuque: William C. Brown.

Vealey, Robin. 1986. Imagery training for performance enhancement. In *Applied sport psychology* by Jean Williams (ed.). Palo Alto: Mayfield Publishing Co.

Vernacchia, Ralph, Rick McGuire, and David Cook. 1996. *Coaching mental excellence.* Portola Valley, Calif.: Warde Publishers.

index

Note: Tables are indicated by an italicized *t* following the page number, figures by an italicized *f*.

about the author

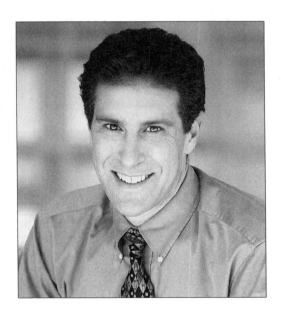

Dean Hinitz is considered the leading authority on bowling psychology. He works with several elite competitors, including many champions in the Professional Bowling Association and the Professional Women's Bowling Association. Hinitz is also a regular guest speaker at the highly regarded International Bowling Academy Super Schools and writes a monthly column for *Bowling This Month*. He is a member of the Nevada State Board of Psychological Examiners and the Nevada State Psychological Association.

Hinitz received his undergraduate degree at the University of Minnesota and his PhD in psychology at the University of Nevada. He resides in Reno, Nevada, with his wife April Bay-Hinitz. He is the chief of psychology at West Hills Hospital in Reno.

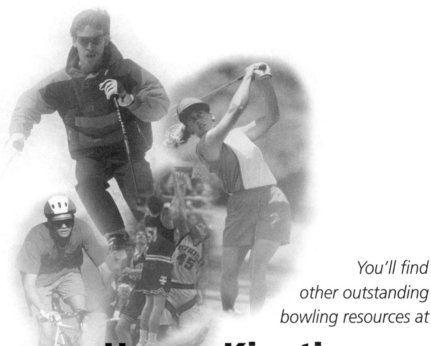